No
Doubt

clearwater crossing

No
Doubt

laura peyton roberts

BANTAM BOOKS
NEW YORK • TORONTO • LONDON • SYDNEY • AUCKLAND

RL 5.8, age 12 and up
NO DOUBT
A Bantam Book / August 1999

ISBN 0-553-49261-6

Published simultaneously in the United States and Canada.

Bantam Books are published by Bantam Books, a division of Random
House, Inc. Its trademark, consisting of the words "Bantam Books" and
the portrayal of a rooster, is Registered in U.S. Patent and Trademark
Office and in other countries. Marca Registrada. Bantam Books, 1540
Broadway, New York, New York 10036.

PRINTED IN THE UNITED STATES OF AMERICA

OPM   10   9   8   7   6   5   4   3   2   1

For Mimi

Be merciful to those who doubt.

Jude 1:22

One

Melanie Andrews reached her front door and turned to wave at the car that had just dropped her off. "Good-bye. Thanks again!"

"Bye, Melanie," Leah called back. "See you at school tomorrow."

Alone now in the backseat of the Rosenthals' big Ford, Nicole Brewster stared at her knees as Mrs. Rosenthal backed out of the Andrewses' driveway. She wanted nothing less than to go to school on Wednesday, but short of breaking a leg or something equally spectacular, she knew there was no way out of it. Maybe if she hadn't already been in trouble for TP'ing that house with her younger sister, Heather, she could have wangled an extra day off to recover from her trip. But considering that she was supposed to be grounded for two weeks beginning the moment she got home from the U.S. Girls contest, her parents weren't likely to accept an excuse.

Whatever, Nicole thought unhappily. Under the circumstances, being grounded didn't even seem like that much punishment. With her modeling dreams so recently shattered, it might be a relief to lock herself away in her bedroom for a couple of weeks and not talk to anybody.

There was no one Nicole could tell about the past weekend's disastrous experiences in California anyway. Certainly not her family—Heather would laugh at her and her mother would know that, once again, her oldest daughter had failed to measure up. The night before, in Hollywood, Nicole had been crushed enough to share some of her troubles with Guy Vaughn, who had been staying in the same hotel, but that had been a one-time thing. She would never want to look so pathetic in front of her real friends.

Especially not Courtney. Nicole barely suppressed a groan as Leah's mother drove relentlessly down the streets toward her house. She wanted desperately to make up the fight she'd had with her best friend, but her spirits were low enough already without crawling for Courtney's forgiveness.

Sighing, she stared out the car window at the storm clouds mantling the sky. The gray Missouri weather made a sharp contrast to the past three days of California sunshine, but it was definitely more in keeping with her mood.

"Is this your street, Nicole?" Mrs. Rosenthal asked as she reached the final turn.

"Yeah. Thanks."

Nicole had managed to get dropped off last, after

Jenna Conrad and Melanie, but now the car was nearly at her house. Every second brought her closer to the inevitable showdown with her parents.

Mrs. Rosenthal pulled into the Brewsters' driveway. "Leah, help Nicole with her luggage," she said, keeping the engine running.

"That's okay. I can get it," Nicole said quickly.

"Yeah, right." Leah laughed as she climbed out to help.

Together they relieved the trunk of Nicole's two suitcases, three tote bags, and assorted loose items. As part of her plan to be discovered as a model in Los Angeles, Nicole had brought nearly as much luggage as the other three girls put together.

A lot of good it did me, she thought morosely. The only attention she'd received from the modeling judges at the U.S. Girls contest had been anything but positive. No one else had even noticed her.

"I think that's all of it," Leah said, setting the last tote bag on Nicole's front doorstep. "See you tomorrow."

"Okay. And thank your mom again for driving us from the airport. I wish you'd won the contest."

Leah's smile grew a little wider. "I don't. Everything turned out fine, so please don't worry about me."

"If you say so."

Even as disillusioned with modeling as Nicole was personally, she still couldn't believe how well Leah was taking losing. She waved good-bye as Leah and her mom drove away, wondering if she would ever really understand the girl.

After the car had disappeared, Nicole hesitated a minute, steeling herself to face her parents. Then, drawing a deep breath, she reached for her front doorknob. Before she could turn it, though, the door opened from within and she stood face to face with her mother.

Mrs. Brewster's pale blond hair was piled high on her head. Her jewel-blue eyes were aggressively outlined in black. "What are you doing standing around out here in the cold?" she demanded. "Why don't you come in?"

"I just got here," Nicole protested. "Geez."

"Don't get smart with me," her mother warned, reaching for a suitcase and pulling it into the entryway. "Your father and I have been waiting for you for the last hour."

Yippee, thought Nicole, grabbing the handle of her other suitcase and carrying that through the door as well. Inside, the furnace made a muffled roar, but the heated air pouring through the wall vents felt good on her cold fingers.

"Leave everything by the stairs," Mrs. Brewster directed, coming back for a couple of tote bags. "Your father and I want to talk to you right now."

"It's a good thing I don't need to use the bathroom," Nicole grumbled as she followed her mother. After her four-hour flight from California and the

4

two-hour drive from St. Louis to Clearwater Crossing, it seemed like her parents could have postponed the thrill of grounding her five minutes longer.

In the living room, Mr. Brewster was sitting in his favorite chair by the fire. Nicole started to head toward the sofa, but, not wanting to risk having her mother sit beside her, decided on the chair across from her father instead.

Mrs. Brewster took the sofa. "The first thing we want to tell you," she said, sitting forward on the cushions, "is that we've decided not to ground you after all."

"Excuse me?"

"We've decided that restricting you doesn't accomplish a thing," Nicole's father confirmed. "It doesn't undo your mischief with Heather, and it doesn't teach you responsibility, either."

"Oh." Nicole supposed she ought to feel grateful, but, having already made up her mind to lie low for a while, she didn't much care anymore whether she was grounded or not.

"You're sixteen now," her mother reminded her, as if Nicole might have somehow forgotten. "Plenty old enough to grow up and start taking responsibility for your actions."

"Oh."

Now that Nicole was thinking about it, she *did* kind of need to use the bathroom—to wash her hands, if nothing else. The meal they had served on the airplane had consisted entirely of finger foods, and the flight attendants had run out of those little wet napkins in the tinfoil packages. As her mother rambled over the old, familiar ground about what a disappointment she was, Nicole used a fingernail on her right hand to clean the nails of her left, flicking the results into space. According to her mother, she was spoiled, ungrateful, immature, selfish—the list went on with the usual charges. Without glancing up, Nicole switched over and began working on the nails of her right hand.

Mrs. Brewster finally paused for air, giving her husband a chance to jump in again.

"So we've decided that the best way to teach you to be more responsible," Mr. Brewster said, "is to give you a chance to make amends for the childish things you've done lately. It's too late to make you clean up the yard you toilet-papered, but remember that crystal vase you broke on New Year's Eve? There's no reason you can't replace it with your own money, just as any responsible person would do."

If her father had managed to grab more of her attention than her mother had, it was only because he was making her laugh. The crystal vase she'd stumbled into in that tipsy haze had cost several hundred dollars, and Nicole didn't have anywhere near that kind of money. What were her parents going to do? Garnish her allowance from now until she was twenty? She shook her head slightly, convinced she had never heard an emptier threat.

"Why can't you be more like your cousin Gail?" Mrs. Brewster asked.

Okay, here we go, Nicole thought, not bothering to disguise her sigh. Gail's name always came up sooner or later in any discussion of responsibility.

Gail Brewster—aka Miss Completely Perfect—was both Nicole's father's brother's daughter and Nicole's least favorite relative. When the two girls were little, Nicole hadn't borne her cousin any particular ill will. But as they had grown and Gail's star had burned brighter and brighter, Nicole had learned to hate her. Gail this, Gail that—she'd heard it all her life. The only saving grace was that Gail lived over in Mapleton, so for the last couple of years Nicole had managed to avoid seeing her except at a few mandatory family events.

"We want you to be more responsible, like Gail," her father said, making Nicole grit her teeth. She was used to having her mother dress her down, but it was harder to take from him.

"Gail never misbehaves," her mother informed her. "And *Gail* has a job."

"Goody for Gail," Nicole shot back. "*I* have a life."

"That's exactly the type of sarcasm—" her mother began.

"Well, now you have a life *and* a job," Mr. Brewster said. "The restaurant Gail works at is owned by a friend of your uncle Dan's. I asked him to put in a good word for you, and since your cousin is such a model employee, it was enough to get you hired sight unseen."

"You . . . what?" Nicole gasped.

"No need to thank us," said her father. "When you get older, you'll realize what a miracle it is to get a job so easily. In the meantime you can show your gratitude by working hard and not embarrassing us."

"My *what*?"

"You start tomorrow after school," her mother said, rising from the sofa. "Now go unpack that luggage. You have some serious laundry to do."

"Your dad won't be home from work for another couple of hours," Leah's mother said, unlocking the front door of their condominium. "We'll have dinner then, but in the meantime you might as well take a breather. Have a bath or something."

"Uh-huh." Dropping her suitcase by the door, Leah headed directly for the answering machine on the kitchen counter.

She had really hoped Miguel would be there when her plane landed in St. Louis. He would have had to cut a day of school to do it, though, so when he hadn't appeared at the airport she had tried not to be disappointed. But now it was late, and school was over. So why wasn't the message light blinking?

He's waiting for me to call him, she decided. Miguel was still intimidated enough by her parents that he wasn't likely to call her house unless he was sure she was home. *Especially now.* She hadn't told her parents about his marriage proposal, but Miguel had no way of knowing that.

"No calls?" she asked her mother.

"You can see a flashing light as well as I can."

"I meant before you left."

"None for you."

Leah reached for the phone, then changed her mind. What she wanted to tell Miguel was better said in person. "Can I borrow the car?"

"Now? You didn't get enough miles in today?"

"I just want to drop by Miguel's for a minute. Please? I really missed him."

"Ah, young love," Mrs. Rosenthal teased, handing over the keys. "Don't be late for dinner."

"Thanks, Mom."

Leah kissed her mother on the cheek as she grabbed the keys and headed out the door, ignoring the gibe about love. Her parents would find out how much she loved Miguel soon enough, when everything was settled.

Driving down the darkening streets to his house, Leah kept a lookout for patches of ice. Her heart beat

9

faster with every mile, and by the time she turned the last corner her hands were slick on the wheel. She couldn't wait to see him, to throw herself into his arms . . .

Except that Miguel's car wasn't parked in its usual place under the streetlight, and when Leah knocked on the del Rioses' door it was his younger sister, Rosa, who answered.

"Hi, Rosa," Leah said, doing her best to keep the disappointment out of her voice. "Miguel's not around?"

Rosa shook her head, her black hair swinging. "Working—so's my mom. Hey, I'm sorry about the modeling contest. Either those judges were blind or your competition was superhuman."

So at least Miguel had gotten *her* message. When Leah and Jenna had phoned home on Monday night, they'd asked Jenna's mom to call Peter with the contest results, so he could let the other guys know.

"Thanks, but I'm over it." Leah hesitated, then blurted out the question she was dying to ask. "Didn't Miguel leave a message for me?"

"Uh, no. Should he have?"

"Well, I just thought, um . . . never mind." It was clear from Rosa's expression that she didn't have a clue about their big news. "Do you know where he's working? Is he still painting the same building as last week?"

"No. They started a new one today, but I don't know where it is. Downtown somewhere."

"Downtown," Leah repeated dully. That covered a lot of ground. "Well . . . ask him to call me when he gets home, all right?"

Rosa nodded. "I'll tell him."

Leah climbed back into the car, full of conflicting emotions. *He'll call me after work*, she reassured herself. *It's not that big a deal.*

But it felt like one. With such an important question pending between them, shouldn't Miguel have been dying to talk to her? Wasn't hearing her answer more important than working?

Apparently not, she thought, pulling away from the curb.

And there was no denying that the realization took the edge off her excitement.

"You're home!" Jenna exclaimed, pulling the Conrads' interior garage door open to greet Caitlin. From the vantage point of the living room window, she'd been watching for her older sister for the last half hour, hoping to talk to her before anyone else got the chance.

Caitlin glanced her way, then grabbed a rumpled towel off a hook on the garage wall and began drying her dog, Abby. Keeping her back to Jenna, she rubbed the dog's muddy paws one by one.

11

"You're off work late today," Jenna tried again.

Caitlin didn't reply.

"Aren't you?" Jenna prompted, a little less hopefully.

"I'm still angry with you, Jenna, if that's what you're trying to find out." Caitlin stood up abruptly and threw the damp towel over its hook. "Come on, Abby."

Pushing past Jenna in the open doorway, Caitlin headed for the staircase, Abby at her heels. Jenna paused only long enough to close the door against the frigid outside air before she hurried to catch her sister.

"Okay. That's fair enough," she said, huffing at Caitlin's pace. "You have every right to be mad. At least you're talking to me now."

"Not really."

Caitlin turned at the landing and headed up the second flight of stairs to the third-floor bedroom the two girls shared.

"Cat, I'm so, so sorry about what I did," Jenna apologized, right behind her. "It was practically all I thought about the entire time I was gone."

Caitlin strode through their open bedroom door and pointed to the lilac dog bed in the corner. Abby went straight to it and lay down.

Jenna ran forward to her own bed. "Look! I brought you something from Los Angeles. It's a Fire & Water T-shirt."

She extended the blue-green bundle eagerly across the strip of hardwood floor between her single bed and her sister's. The shirt had been rolled like a fat sausage, a curly yellow ribbon cinching its middle.

But instead of being excited, Caitlin looked as if it might bite her. Finally she reached out a hand to take it.

"Thanks," she said, tossing the shirt onto the ledge behind her bed. She peeled off her coat and sweatshirt, then headed for the closet.

"Where are you going?"

"To shower." Caitlin grabbed her things and walked out of the room.

"Great," Jenna moaned, dropping onto her bed.

She was completely determined to make up with her sister, and she had done her very best, but so far their reconciliation hadn't gone nearly as well as she'd hoped. Depressed by her failure, Jenna tried to focus on the positive.

At least she's talking to me. And she didn't lock herself in the bathroom again. Well, at least not right away.

If only she hadn't blabbed to Peter about Caitlin's crush on his brother, David! Would it really have killed her to keep her mouth shut, like Caitlin had asked her to?

Jenna sighed, dying to know if there had been any further developments in the David situation while she'd been gone, but her questions on that front would clearly have to wait—maybe forever.

"Caitlin! Peter's here!" ten-year-old Sarah hollered from downstairs. A second later the doorbell rang.

Jenna grabbed a second Fire & Water shirt and headed for the door. "Let him in," she shouted, thundering down the stairs.

Peter was alone in the entryway when she got there, a smile on his face and a shock of dark blond hair falling across his eyes.

"Peter!" she cried, running forward. "Wow, it's good to see you! You look . . . amazing."

She blushed, belatedly embarrassed by her own enthusiasm, but Peter just reached to hug her.

"I missed you."

"You too! You have no idea how many times I wished you were in Los Angeles. It would have been so much more fun."

She grabbed his elbow and pulled him into the den. "Come and see what I brought you." Dropping onto the sofa beside him, she pushed the T-shirt into his hands.

Peter pulled off the yellow ribbon, unfurling the shirt across his lap. "Cool! Thanks, Jenna."

"I got me and Caitlin ones just like it, so we'll have to coordinate to make sure we don't all wear them on the same day."

Not that that's too likely. Caitlin would have to look at hers first, and she'd made it pretty clear she had no interest in doing that. *Not while she's still mad, at least.*

14

Jenna glanced at both doorways into the den to make sure none of her sisters was around, then lowered her voice anyway. Anyone who took chances in a house with five girls was a fool.

"Did you ask David why he wants to write to Mary Beth yet?" she whispered.

David's letter to Caitlin requesting Mary Beth's college address had been the key to Jenna's undoing. Only shortly before the letter arrived, Jenna had learned that Caitlin was hiding practically a lifelong crush on David. Between Caitlin's shyness and the fact that David was away at college, however, romance hadn't seemed likely. Then, completely unexpectedly, David had written to Caitlin. Caitlin's—and Jenna's—hopes had soared, only to be dashed again when it had turned out that the only thing David wanted was their oldest sister's address. Caitlin had been devastated. She'd begged Jenna not to tell anyone, but, wanting to help, Jenna had eventually spilled the story to Peter, hoping to learn the nature of David's interest in Mary Beth. And, unfortunately, Caitlin had caught her in the act.

Now Peter shook his head. "You didn't want me to send an e-mail, and I almost never call him at school. I couldn't think of a good enough excuse to—"

"That's okay," Jenna said quickly. She was still dying to know David's intentions, but with Caitlin already so mad at her, she didn't want to risk making the situation worse.

15

"Listen," she whispered. "Caitlin heard me talking to you on the phone before I left, and she's really mad at me for not keeping her secret."

"Oh no," Peter groaned. "Poor Caitlin."

Poor Caitlin! Jenna thought. *What about poor me?*

But Peter was right. Caitlin was the one whose trust had been betrayed; Jenna's problems were her own fault.

"I know. And I'm doing my best to make up with her, but it isn't going too well. The last thing I need right now is to give her more ammunition, so you'd better forget about talking to David."

The relief in Peter's blue eyes was obvious. "With pleasure!" he exclaimed, sinking back into the couch.

He looked far too relaxed to suit Jenna.

"At least for now," she added.

Two

"Okay, so where is he?" Melanie muttered nervously, peering through the crowd left in the hallway.

Most of the students had already poured out the doorway she was standing beside on their way to eat lunch in the cafeteria, but Melanie still hadn't caught even a glimpse of Jesse.

"He has to be coming out this door," she whispered. "He *always* comes out this door."

Ben Pipkin suddenly appeared from around a corner and headed directly toward her. Melanie felt conspicuous, aware that her loitering was becoming more and more obvious as the crowd thinned out, but she held her ground anyway.

"Hey, Melanie!" Ben greeted her. "You're back!"

"We got back yesterday, but school was already out by then. Not that any of us found missing a day of classes too tragic."

"You're so lucky. Between yesterday and the Monday holiday, you only have a three-day week."

Melanie nodded, barely listening. "Have you seen Jesse today, by any chance?"

"I saw him by the parking lot this morning. Why? What's up?"

"Nothing's up. I just want to talk to him."

"What about?"

"Who are you? The FBI?"

Ben turned red. "I didn't mean to be nosy."

"I know. I'm sorry. It's just . . . I'm in a hurry, all right? You don't know where he is now?"

"No, but if I see him in the cafeteria I'll tell him you're looking for him."

"Thanks."

Ben started out the door.

"No, Ben! Wait. Don't tell him anything."

"All right," he said slowly, as if she were crazy.

"Don't look at me like that. I just want to find him myself."

Ben nodded, went through the doorway, and struck off across the quad to the cafeteria.

Good one, Melanie thought, watching him go. The way the wind was blowing outside, scrawny Ben looked as if he might be swept along with the dead leaves and torn paper bags that swirled through the paved rectangle. He made it to the cafeteria, however, and disappeared through the large double doors. *Now Ben thinks I'm a lunatic.*

Maybe she was. That was the simplest—if not the most likely—explanation for her sudden, intense desire to reunite with Jesse. After she'd told him there was nothing real between them, after she'd coldly returned the porcelain angel he'd given her for Christmas, lunacy was a possibility she couldn't rule out. And then there was the evidence of the clothes she was wearing. Looking down at the outfit it had taken her nearly an hour to select, she shook her head. Would any *sane* person wear a short skirt in such wind?

The hall was essentially empty. Melanie buttoned her coat and opened the door Ben had just gone through. Maybe Jesse had gotten past her somehow and was already in the cafeteria.

Or maybe he's out in his car, she thought, hesitating with her hand still on the door. She had seen him out there on other days, listening to CDs and kicking back in his leather seat. It seemed awfully cold to be hanging out in the parking lot, but knowing Jesse he'd just run the engine and blast the heater. Turning abruptly, Melanie began walking through the deserted main building toward the front of the school and the student parking lot. *Even if he's not there, if I see his car I'll know he's around.*

The frigid wind that had been swirling through the protected quad gusted with three times more strength in the open parking lot. Melanie would have turned back halfway across the lawn if she hadn't seen Jesse's bright red car parked at the edge of the pavement. When she got closer, however, she realized he wasn't in it. She almost ran for the building again, but then she had a thought: In case she didn't find Jesse, maybe she should leave him a note. Swinging her backpack off her shoulder, she found a scrap of paper.

Jesse, call me. Melanie, she scribbled, bracing the scrap against her knee.

Tucking the note under his windshield wiper, she began to walk off, but a moment later she was back again. What if the wind blew it away? What if those storm clouds finally opened up and the rain melted the ink? What if someone else came along and took it? If Jesse didn't call her, how would she know if he just didn't get her note?

What if the world comes to an end tomorrow? she asked herself sarcastically, aware she was being more than a little ridiculous. Even so, she snatched the note from under the wiper, crumpled it up, and put it in her coat pocket.

I'd rather talk to him in person anyway, she decided, stalking off to look in the gym.

Miguel sat at the end of an empty table and slapped his lunch tray down in front of him. "So what do you think?" he asked Leah as she slid onto the bench across from his. "Is it going to rain before sixth period, or will it wait until tonight?"

"Huh? I don't know."

Why did he even care about the weather when they had so many other, more important, things to discuss?

"It was nasty the whole time you were gone," he said, digging into his meat loaf. "All I could think about was how nice and warm you must be in California."

Funny, all I could think about was whether or not I was going to marry you.

Leah picked up a fork and poked at the unappetizing food, actually eating it the last thing on her mind.

"So, lots of sun, huh?" he asked.

"Yeah, it was sunny. I thought we covered that." Her voice came out sharper than she had intended, but enough was enough.

What in the world is he thinking?

When Miguel had finally called her at nine o'clock the night before, all he had wanted to talk about was his job and the U.S. Girls contest. Leah had tried to listen patiently to his description of the building he was painting, and she had explained twice that she was *happy* she hadn't won the modeling contest. But every time she had tried to steer the conversation around to his marriage proposal, Miguel had begun talking of the weather— exactly the way he was doing now. When she had finally come out and said she was ready to answer his question, amazingly he had put her off, asking her to wait to tell him in person. But now here they were, in person, and Leah didn't know what his excuse was anymore.

"We sure haven't seen much snow yet this—"

"Miguel, I thought we were going to talk."

He put down his milk and glanced nervously around the cafeteria. "Yeah, but not here. It's too crowded."

There were the usual number of people in the cafeteria, but Leah and Miguel had the end of the table to themselves. Besides, no one even two feet away could have possibly heard what they were saying over the din of competing conversations. "No one is listening."

"I just . . . not here, all right?" he pleaded.

"Why not? I don't know what the big deal—"

"Ben! Hey, Ben!" Miguel called suddenly, half standing to wave Ben over. "Hey, there's an empty seat right here next to Leah."

Leah stared at her boyfriend, speechless, but Ben was already at her side, eagerly taking Miguel up on his offer.

"Thanks," he said, sliding in with his tray. "Hi, Leah. How was Los Angeles? I mean, uh, I'm sorry you didn't win, but did you have a nice time other than that?"

Not that stupid contest again! Leah wanted to scream. "It was fine," she said through gritted teeth. "Los Angeles was fine."

"I'll bet you hated coming back to weather like this after all that California sunshine."

Not the weather again!

But Ben had cleared the way, and Miguel was off and running with his new favorite subject. "Do you think it's going to rain soon?"

Ben looked hugely pleased to be consulted on something so important. "It's hard to say," he opined, setting his Jell-O wiggling with one finger. "Maybe not until tonight."

Leah listened in disbelief as the guys discussed every detail of that day's weather, followed by expected highlights for the rest of the week. She couldn't believe she was sitting directly across a table from the guy she loved, from the guy she was ready to *marry*, and all he wanted to do was talk about the weather. With Ben!

The end-of-lunch bell rang.

"Wow, is that the bell already?" Ben exclaimed. "Lunch sure goes by fast!"

"It did today," said Leah, staring her boyfriend down. *Invite him to walk with us and you're dead.*

Ben stood up and grabbed his backpack. "Sorry I can't hang out, but I've got to run. I still have gym this period and . . . well, it's just better not to be late."

Leah waved distractedly, not watching him leave.

"Meet me after school," she told Miguel. "We'll take a drive or something, and we'll be *totally* alone."

23

Miguel picked up his things, and they both started walking.

"I can't today. I have to work."

"Again? You worked yesterday!"

He made a face. "I don't make up the schedule. Besides, it's all good money."

"Well, what *is* the schedule?" Leah demanded. "I can't figure out what days you're supposed to work and what days you aren't."

Out in the quad, an icy wind was blowing. Leah started to head for the main building, but Miguel didn't follow.

"I go the other way now, remember?" he said, pointing toward the southern classroom buildings.

"Oh. Right." Since their schedules had changed for the second semester, they didn't even have fifth period together anymore. "So what's the story, Miguel? I want to see you. We need to talk."

Miguel shrugged. "I already know what you're going to say. Why can't we just forget I ever asked?"

Before she could form a reply, he strode off toward the classrooms on the other side of the quad, leaving her speechless behind him.

After all the soul-searching she'd been through, he was taking his proposal back? He didn't even want to talk about it?

He does not *know what I'm going to say*, Leah thought, watching him disappear in the crowd. *If anything he ought to think . . .*

24

That's it! she realized, relieved.

No wonder Miguel was acting so strangely. No wonder all he wanted to do was work and talk about the weather.

Of course he doesn't want to hear my answer—he thinks I'm going to turn him down!

This stinks! Nicole thought angrily, sinking lower in the cold bus seat. *I can't believe I'm doing this.*

The instant school had let out that Wednesday, she'd had to run straight to the bus. Between all the stupid stops and the transfer she had to make, it was a half-hour ride just to get to her new job at the boundary between Clearwater Crossing and Mapleton—and her mother had made it clear how much trouble she'd be in if she ever arrived at work late. Nicole hadn't even had time to find Courtney and explain what was going on before she'd had to leave.

Not that Courtney was speaking to her.

Nicole sighed. *She's never going to start speaking to me, either, if I don't find a way to break the ice.*

But that day at school she'd never seen her best friend alone. Every time she'd caught sight of her, Courtney had shot her a haughty look from the safety of someone else's company, and at lunch she'd purposely sat with a bunch of people Nicole barely knew. Kissing up was embarrassing enough without doing it in front of strangers.

25

Except that now she's going to think that I'm avoiding her . . .

The bus stopped for the ten millionth time, and with a jolt Nicole realized that it had finally reached her corner. Grabbing the straps of her backpack, she hurried up the center aisle, the overly detailed instructions her mother had given her clutched in her other hand.

"Thanks," she muttered to the driver as she walked past him and down the steps to the icy sidewalk. The bus pulled away again, leaving Nicole alone.

She checked the note in her hand. Her mother had mapped her whole route out for her, down to the exact number of stops each of the two buses would make, but Nicole didn't feel any gratitude. Far from it.

If they want me to do this stupid job, the least they could do is let me drive one of their cars, she thought. The bus ride would waste an additional hour of her life on every day she worked, and she wouldn't get paid one extra penny for traveling. For the four hours of her shift, she'd get only minimum wage—except that today she wasn't getting paid at all because she was just there to check in, meet the manager, pick up her uniform, and fill out some paperwork before she started for real on Thursday.

This stinks, she thought again.

According to her mother's map, the restaurant

was on the corner just ahead. *It must be on the other side of this building*, Nicole decided, beginning to walk faster. The bus had let her out in front of a big drugstore, but she could see a stretch of pavement between it and the next corner. Maybe a parking lot . . .

She reached the end of the drugstore and stopped dead in her tracks. The sight before her was so heinous, so in excess of her very worst nightmares, that all she could do was stand and stare.

WIENERAGEOUS, the sign over the shoe box of a building proclaimed in blue-and-orange neon. A pink neon arrow pointed from the sign down to the sloping roof, which was painted in red-and-white checkerboard squares. The exterior walls sported vertical stripes of pink and purple, with a continuous, canary yellow board making a bright horizontal break between them and the edge of the roof. A few deserted tables with orange fiberglass umbrellas occupied a small concrete slab out front; a single-lane drive-through looped around the other three sides of the building.

"This is *not* happening," Nicole begged under her breath. Wienerageous was the most aggressively ugly fast-food dive she'd ever seen. She approached it cautiously, one step at a time, hoping it was a mirage.

The name wasn't bad enough? she wailed silently as she inched forward. *Look at this place! I can't tell Courtney I'm working here—she'll give me grief for the rest of my life!*

27

Nicole was almost to the front door when it opened suddenly from within. An employee was coming outside, a full plastic trash bag in one hand. The girl stopped when she saw Nicole and held the door open wide.

"Welcome to Wienerageous, where our smiles are contagious!" she said with a big grin.

Nicole could only stare. The poor girl was wearing the most hideous, the most *embarrassing* uniform Nicole had ever seen. The garish interior of the little restaurant swam out of focus as Nicole tried to take in the fact that she might have to wear one just like it.

"Tell me the truth," she whispered desperately. "Do they *make* you say that to the customers?"

The girl glanced around her, then shrugged. "I didn't think it up on my own."

Despite the fact that the door was still being held for her, letting all the warm air in the restaurant out into the cold, Nicole stood paralyzed in the doorway, her entire social life passing before her eyes. She pictured herself wearing that horrendous outfit, saying that ridiculous slogan to total strangers, and her mind boggled.

Then she imagined having to say it to someone she knew and nearly burst into tears.

She took a faltering step inside, just one thought in her head: *No one can ever find out I'm working here. No one. Never, ever, ever!*

28

* * *

"Why don't I take the ladder and start spraying the ceilings?" Miguel suggested. "I'll start in that back room and see how far forward I can get."

His supervisor, Sabrina Ambrosi, frowned. "You did the ceilings last time, Miguel. Give yourself a break and let Phil work the ladder."

"I don't mind," he said, picking up the ladder anyway.

"I mind—and last time I checked I was still in charge." Sabrina turned and yelled back into the echoing office building. "Hey, Phil, come on. You're on the ladder tonight."

Phil and Eddie, his usual partner in crime, appeared, Eddie scratching the beer belly beneath his paint-spattered T-shirt.

"Why can't Miguel work the ladder?" Phil asked. "He likes it."

Miguel leaned against the wall to hear Sabrina's answer, knowing she would have one. Phil and Eddie were both in their mid-twenties, years older than Sabrina, but she faced them down with cool violet eyes, not in the least intimidated. Her father had given Sabrina her position as supervisor because he owned the construction company; she kept it because she was good at what she did.

"I need Miguel to do the door frames. Whoever did them last time got gloss all over the flat."

Everyone knew Phil had done them last time.

Eddie scratched his belly a little faster, but Phil just reached for the ladder. Miguel handed it over and went to get a can of gloss from the company truck. He couldn't care less what task Sabrina assigned him so long as he got to do it alone. The last thing he needed with all the things already on his mind was someone yakking his ear off.

Picking the most remote office in the building, Miguel pried the lid off the paint can and got busy. Most days he didn't mind painting, but that evening he was actually looking forward to it. There was nothing tricky about painting, nothing to figure out or explain. He dipped the brush into the thick white liquid and began stroking it down the door frame, being extra careful not to let it drip from the wood onto the walls, which had been sprayed flat white the night before.

He could have told Phil that Sabrina would bust him for that kind of sloppiness. That was just how she worked. Sometimes the other guys would whine behind her back about how picky she was, but Miguel never did. At least with Sabrina, a guy always knew where he stood. There were no guessing games involved.

Unlike with Leah, he thought with a sigh.

He could still barely believe he'd proposed to her. Leaving work on Friday with that half-baked excuse about a family emergency, driving like a maniac all the way to St. Louis, going down on his knee in the middle of the airport . . . It all seemed like a dream now.

Except for the part where Leah had said no.

He couldn't even remember anymore what had made him think she might say yes. The whole idea had been stupid. He just loved her so much, and she had been so upset by the idea of their being separated. For the heat of a few brief hours, marriage had seemed like a possibility. Now he was sorry he'd ever mentioned it.

Why didn't I think it out more? he berated himself.

At the time it had seemed imperative to ask her before she left for Los Angeles. If Leah had won the modeling contest and he had asked her afterward, she might have thought he was only doing it out of fear of losing her, or because he wanted to ride on her glory somehow.

Nothing could be farther from the truth. He was thrilled she *hadn't* won. She had never wanted to be a model anyway, and the more he'd thought about the consequences of her becoming one, the less he had liked the idea. He only wished now that he'd had some way of knowing in advance that she wasn't going to win. Maybe he'd have acted with more common sense.

Not that he wouldn't have been thrilled if she'd said yes. She could have sent him home from St. Louis the happiest guy on Earth.

But instead she'd told him he couldn't be serious,

31

that they were too young, his proposal too sudden. He'd practically had to beg her to think it over just to keep her from saying no on the spot. Her protests had been the same as no, though—he didn't need a degree from one of her fancy colleges to figure that much out. And he'd give anything not to hear her say it again.

You are such a fool, he thought, smoothing the paint he'd just put down until the brush strokes disappeared.

He'd laid his heart bare for the entire world to see—and if Leah hadn't exactly trampled on it, she'd simply stepped over it and continued on her way. He had never felt more stupid. And that wasn't even the worst part.

He felt like nothing would ever be the same between them again.

Three

"How about passing the milk down here?" Jenna's next-youngest sister, Maggie, demanded at the breakfast table on Thursday.

"Yeah, Jenna," seventh-grader Allison chimed in. "You're hogging."

"I am not. I'm just sitting here eating my cereal. *Trying* to eat my cereal," Jenna amended as Maggie stood up and reached across her to get the carton.

"Jenna's not a hog. The hogs are having seconds." Sarah's observation earned her dirty looks from Maggie and Allison, but Jenna flashed her youngest sister a big smile.

"You girls knock it off," Mrs. Conrad said from the end of the table, where she sat flipping through the newspaper while the four youngest members of her family bickered. Mr. Conrad and Caitlin had already left for work, Caitlin sneaking out before Jenna was even awake. "If you keep this up you'll all be late for school."

Jenna grabbed her orange juice and started gulping. Peter was picking her up that morning, and she

33

wanted to have time to brush her teeth before he got there. She finished, dropping her dishes in the sink before she bolted upstairs to the bathroom. She was still spitting toothpaste when Peter's horn sounded in the driveway.

"Jenna!" two or three voices called from downstairs.

"I know! I hear it!" she yelled back, taking just long enough to put on some lip gloss and swipe a brush through her hair one last time.

Her backpack was on the landing. She snagged it as she ran past, attacking the stairs two by two.

"Bye, Mom," she called, slamming the front door behind her.

Peter had turned his car around and parked at the curb. She ran to it, slowing her steps only enough to avoid slipping on the icy walkway.

He was laughing when she opened the passenger door. "Take your time. I think we're going to make it."

"You think, but you don't *know*," she countered cheerfully. Still, from his reaction she couldn't help wondering if she looked like some kind of wild woman. She could imagine her hair flying every which way and her cheeks turning pink in the cold. There was a time she would have told herself that something like that didn't matter, that it was only her and Peter, but now Peter was the person she cared about impressing most. She buckled her seat belt, then checked the mirror on the passenger visor to make sure her mad dash out the door hadn't undone whatever good she'd just accomplished in the bathroom.

"You're in a good mood this morning," Peter said as he drove away from the curb. "Did you and Caitlin make up?"

"I wish! No, I'm just happy to see you. Caitlin's still barely putting up with me."

"Did you tell her you were sorry?"

"Only about a million times." Flipping the visor up, Jenna fell back into her seat. "She nods and says okay, but I can tell it isn't. She's really furious."

"Well, you can't exactly blame her."

"I know, I know. Don't rub it in."

"I'm not rubbing it in. I'm just saying that after what happened, maybe telling Caitlin you're sorry isn't going to be enough. Maybe you're going to have to show her."

"Show her?" Jenna repeated skeptically. "How am I supposed to do that?"

Peter shrugged slightly, his hands still on the wheel. "That's up to you, I guess. You know your sister better than I do."

"If only we could fix her up with David!" Jenna said, imagining what a hero she'd be then. "*That* would show her."

"I was thinking more like making her a card," Peter replied, alarmed. "You said you were going to leave Caitlin and David alone."

Jenna sighed. "I know."

Peter reached over and squeezed her hand. "We ought to have an Eight Prime meeting. Between the sports equipment we bought the kids during the after-Christmas sales and painting Kurt's name on the bus, the Junior Explorers' savings account is completely broke."

Jenna knew he was only changing the subject to keep from depressing her further, but there was nothing left to say about Caitlin anyway.

"You're right. We said we'd do that after we got back from L.A."

"What kind of fund-raiser should we have this time?"

Jenna shook her head. "Beats me. When should we have the meeting?"

"Next Thursday?" he suggested.

"That's good. It's Thursday today, so that gives people a whole week's notice."

"I hope Miguel can get off work," Peter said. "But if he can't, I guess Leah can cover for him."

"Whose house should we have it at?"

Peter pulled into the CCHS student parking lot and began cruising for a space. "We can always have it at mine. I'm sure my mom won't mind."

"Or we could have it at mine." But even as she spoke, Jenna envisioned Caitlin arriving home late from work, stalking through the den with Abby and giving Jenna the cold shoulder in front of all of her friends. "Or maybe somebody new wants to do it.

Jesse, Miguel, and Ben have never hosted a single meeting. Maybe one of them wants a turn."

Peter found a spot and parked the car. "We can ask. Miguel's house is pretty small. I don't know about Ben's, but Jesse's is huge."

"Well, let's ask him, then," Jenna said. "If he says no, one of us can do it."

The two of them started off across the parking lot toward the high school's wet front lawn.

"Hey, I'm wearing my new T-shirt," Peter told her, unzipping the top few inches of his parka.

Jenna glimpsed the deep blue green of the Fire & Water shirt she had bought him and, although she didn't understand exactly why, her spirits rose at the sight. It just made her feel good to see him wearing a gift she'd picked out and paid for with her own money.

Does he know how I feel? she wondered. *Is that why he wore it?*

She smiled at him before another thought rubbed the grin right off her face.

Caitlin knows. That's why she still hasn't even opened hers.

"I don't know why we couldn't just go to Burger City," Miguel grumbled as he yanked the restaurant door open for Leah. "Or, better still, the cafeteria. It's going to rain again."

"Don't be such a grouch."

37

Leah shrugged off her coat in the warm interior of the restaurant, hoping for an empty table. She had insisted on bringing Miguel to Angelo's because it was both quieter than Burger City and farther from school, which made running into anyone they knew less likely. If they had to wait for a table, however, they'd be late getting back to class. Considering the importance of the occasion, Leah wasn't too worried about picking up a tardy on her otherwise spotless record, but she didn't want to make Miguel any more anxious than he already was.

"There's a booth over there," she said, pointing.

Miguel led the way without a word, his jaw tight with poorly suppressed irritation. They took seats on opposite sides of the table, Miguel's back to a wall and Leah's against the tall bench. She smiled—absolute privacy.

"Can I bring you something to drink?" the waitress asked, appearing with two menus.

"A couple of Cokes," Leah said, waving the menus away. "And we'll both have the spaghetti lunch special."

A glance at Miguel's stony expression made Leah wonder if she should have let him order for himself, but the waitress was already walking off.

"You like spaghetti, right?" she asked.

Miguel shrugged. "Whatever. Leah, if you still feel like you have to tell me something, just hurry up and say it. You don't have to let me down easy. It isn't working anyway."

Leah smiled again, imagining how his attitude was about to change. "All right. Actually, there *is* something I want to tell you. I've been thinking about it, and I've decided that maybe getting married is a good idea."

"What?" Miguel's brown eyes were as stunned as if she'd just slapped him. "You think what?"

"We love each other, don't we? And even though I never expected to get married right out of high school, now I'm asking myself why not. I mean, you can't plan everything in your life. Sometimes things just happen."

Miguel blinked a couple of times. "What about college?"

"What about college?" she repeated, surprised. She had expected him to hug the breath out of her body—or to smile at the very least. Instead he was arguing with her.

"Well?" His eyes bored into hers.

What about *college?* she asked herself. She had planned to let college slide for a while, or maybe even to put that dream aside. But suddenly she couldn't bring herself to say so. The way Miguel was looking at her was so full of uncertainty . . . and the obviousness of his doubts was like a spark that enflamed her own.

"What about a long engagement?" she countered nervously.

"What does that accomplish? The whole point of getting married is to get married *now*, so that we can be together."

"So you're saying it's now or not at all?"

Miguel leaned across the table and grabbed her by both hands. His eyes searched hers intently. Leah was sure he was about to say something important when their waitress reappeared and slammed two dripping Cokes down on the table.

"There you go," she said, wiping her hands on her apron. "Food'll be up in just a minute."

Leah barely glanced the woman's way, but when her eyes returned to Miguel's, the spell was broken. He was leaning back in the booth again, his gaze lost somewhere in space. His hands slid slowly off hers.

"Just . . . don't say anything until you're sure what you want," he said, his voice tired and distant. "Take all the time you need."

Leah opened her mouth to tell him she *was* sure, that she didn't need any more time. But none of those words came out.

She didn't understand why Miguel had suddenly grown so cool on the topic of marriage, but there was one thing she knew for sure: She wasn't about to say yes if *he* was going to say no.

* * *

Melanie gnawed nervously at the edge of a fingernail before she realized what she was doing and snatched it out of her mouth.

That looks real attractive. Shoving her hands into her coat pockets, she glanced back toward the main building to see if Jesse had come out yet. There were so many people outside, it was hard to be sure she hadn't missed him in the crowd, but as long as she stayed by his car, she knew he wasn't leaving without talking to her.

Not today, he isn't.

Despite her best efforts the day before, she had never managed to track Jesse down. After deciding not to leave a note on his car, she'd looked for him in the gym with no success. No one had seen him in the cafeteria, either, and before she'd had a chance to check out the library, the end-of-lunch bell had rung.

Later, she'd caught a distant glimpse of him between classes. He'd looked the same as usual, so it had kind of shocked her the way her heart had raced at the sight of his shorn brown head cresting the wave of hallway traffic. She'd felt almost foolish that Jesse could have such an effect on her, but she'd still considered running down the hallway and throwing herself into his arms. Sixth period had been about to start, though, and the last thing she'd wanted was to appear desperate.

More desperate than she was, anyway. All through

sixth period, her mind had been in a fog. She hadn't heard more than a few words of her English teacher's explication of *Tortilla Flat*, and she hadn't even pretended to take notes on what little she'd heard.

I'll catch him the minute school lets out, she'd promised herself, doodling curlicues in the margin of her notebook. She'd apologize for the way she had acted and hope he wasn't in the mood to harbor a grudge.

But even though she'd run directly to the parking lot the moment class had let out, somehow she'd missed him. Jesse's BMW had been gone.

Her disappointment had been intense, especially after she'd been so psyched up to talk to him. And she couldn't help worrying that the longer she let things go, the more used to living without her he'd get. Now that she knew breaking up with Jesse had been a mistake, she wanted to fix it as soon as possible, before he latched on to someone else.

Or somebody latched on to him. She had almost called him at home that night, but some instinct had made her wait. The only reason Jesse had wanted her in the first place was because she had been hard to get—throwing herself at him now could only hurt her cause.

Melanie shivered in the cold parking lot and resumed scanning for Jesse. *Of course, if I had known I was going to have to wait this long, I might have called him anyway*.

He had managed to elude her all day again, to the

point that she'd begun to think his scarcity was no accident. Was it possible he was avoiding her on purpose? And if so, was that a good sign or a bad one? She patted the cold metal behind her, to reassure herself that Jesse hadn't somehow escaped a second time.

"What are you doing to my car?" a gruff voice demanded. "You'd better not be scratching the paint."

Melanie spun around, startled. "Why would I scratch the paint?" After all her careful surveillance, Jesse had managed to come up behind her somehow.

His expression was hard as he walked around to the driver's side. "How would I know? I obviously have no idea what goes on in your head."

All right, Melanie thought, *I deserved that*. If she wanted to make up with him, she couldn't afford to be offended.

She stepped away from his shiny red paint. "Actually, there's been a lot in my head the last few days. Do you have a minute?"

"No. Charlie's expecting me to take him to the grocery store."

"Oh." She had hoped to invite him to her house, but she could hardly ask him to come over instead of taking an old man shopping for food. "I didn't know you were still seeing Charlie."

After he'd been caught with liquor in his locker, Jesse had been assigned to help a housebound senior citizen as a community service project, but Melanie knew he had already served his forty-hour sentence.

"I guess you don't know everything either, do you?"

"Um, no. Jesse, we need to talk."

Jesse's smile was incredulous and not particularly nice. "*Now* you want to talk? What for?"

"What do you mean, what for? Do I need a reason?"

Jesse looked at her hard, then turned his head away. A muscle twitched at the hinge of his jaw.

He's angry, but he still likes me, she thought, relieved. Everything about his body language said so.

But when his eyes came back to hers, they held no trace of their former fascination.

"Yes," he said coldly. "*You* need a reason."

"Welcome to Wienerageous, where our smiles are contagious," Nicole said through gritted teeth, her eyes half-closed with humiliation.

"Good!" cried her cousin Gail. "Except, don't forget, you have to smile when you say that or it doesn't work at all."

"I'll smile when I say it to customers," Nicole bargained, unable to believe that even a goody-goody like Gail thought that slogan could ever work.

Gail tucked a stray strand of coal black hair behind one ear, rendering her appearance perfect again, and nodded happily. With her milk-white skin and rosy cheeks and lips, Gail reminded Nicole so strongly of Snow White that she half-expected the dwarves to burst in any minute, hungry from a hard day at the mines.

I would have to get trained by Gail, Nicole thought disgustedly, wondering why one of the other employees couldn't have shown her the ropes. The manager, Mr. Roarke, probably thought he was doing her a big favor by letting her train with her cousin, but Nicole would have gladly worked with anyone else—even that pimply little troll behind the grill.

Or wait, maybe that's one of the dwarves.

Gail glanced toward the open door into the hallway, then consulted the training manual on the rickety table between them. "Okay, now tell me our first rule of service."

For the past hour, the girls had been studying in the "break room," a dingy, windowless closet that also served as the changing room for employees. Nicole had used it in that capacity earlier, to put on her newly issued Wienerageous uniform. She looked down at her clothes now and squeezed her eyes shut, horrified.

"Nicole?"

"What?"

"Our first rule of service?"

"Every bite . . . uh . . ."

She opened her eyes just enough to glimpse the affront to fashion she was wearing: a pink-and-orange vertically striped smock top with a red ruffle around the bottom, royal blue polyester bell-bottoms, and black orthopedic shoes. She was only glad there wasn't a mirror in the break room so she didn't have to see her hat. Unfortunately, Gail's was right in front of her, and Nicole could only pretend she wasn't wearing the exact same lavender mushroom.

"Every bite a delight . . . ," Gail prompted patiently.

"Every bite a delight or we'll make it right," Nicole said in a singsong voice, wishing she were dead.

"Okay! That's good! Really good." Gail glanced at the doorway again, then turned the page. "We'll just go over Roarke's Rules one more time, and then you'll be ready to start learning the dining room responsibilities."

Nicole didn't bother to hide her sigh. They'd already been over Roarke's Rules at least a dozen times.

"Question number one!" Gail announced in an obnoxiously perky tone. "Roarke's Rules are also known as . . ."

"The Five Rules of Continued Employment."

"Good! Let's say them together, so I can make sure you've got them." Gail leaned forward with a slightly worried expression. "You're supposed to know them word for word before I let you out of this room," she confided. "But if you only miss a 'the' or an 'and' or something, I can probably let you slide."

"Gee, thanks," Nicole said ungratefully, wondering if such a reckless breach of the rules would keep Gail awake all night. Gail didn't know that Nicole was only working there because she was being punished—Nicole's parents apparently hadn't considered that a selling point when they got their daughter the job—and Nicole could only imagine what the little princess would think if she ever found out her black-sheep cousin had been drinking at a party.

Except even my parents don't know about that. The TP incident she was actually being punished for paled in comparison—although just running around with a few rolls of toilet paper would probably look pretty wild to sheltered Gail.

"Okay, rule one. Ready?" Gail held up one finger.

"Never disrespect a customer, no matter how difficult he or she may be," Nicole and Gail recited in unison.

"Good!" Two fingers.

"Timeliness is next to cleanliness."

Nicole rushed into rule number three before being prompted, eager to end the nightmare of being tutored by Gail.

"Never argue, complain, or discuss breaks, salaries, or other employee business in front of a customer."

"Ooh, you're doing so good!" Gail cooed. "Number four?"

"If you want to progress, take care how you dress."

Nicole found that one particularly rich, given the unabated hideousness of their uniforms, but Gail

47

had already explained it meant an employee's uniform had to be neat and complete at all times—no ditching the hat, in other words.

"And number five?" Gail asked.

"No free food for anyone, ever," they said together.

"Wow, Nicole, that's fantastic! You learned those so fast."

"They're not that difficult," said Nicole, wondering if Gail thought she was stupid.

Probably, she realized. Compared to Gail's straight A's, Nicole's report card didn't exactly shine. *Poor Nicole*, she could imagine her aunt Ellen telling Gail. *You'll have to help her as much as you can, dear. She's not smart like you.*

"You'd be surprised," Gail said, slamming the book shut and standing up. "I've trained a lot of new people, and they don't always catch on real fast."

Nicole stood up too and automatically reached to smooth the wrinkles out of her pants. Her hands touched polyester so stiff and set in its ways that the only crease it would ever see was the one permanently melted into the front and back of each leg, splitting the huge flare down the middle.

"I feel like Cher in these pants," Nicole complained as she followed Gail to the open door.

Gail turned around instantly, her perfectly sculpted black eyebrows raised in silent alarm. "Uh-uh," she scolded gently. "Rule number three."

"There aren't any customers here."

"Four, then."

"If I wasn't *wearing* the pants, you might have a point."

Gail looked just the slightest bit exasperated. "Common sense, then. Mr. Roarke really likes these outfits. He thinks they create an image that makes us stand out."

"We stand out, all right," Nicole retorted the moment Gail stepped through the doorway.

Out in the restaurant, everything was spotless. Even so, two of the three people working behind the counter were wiping down the countertops and equipment with wet towels.

"When no diners are seen, it's time to clean," Gail informed her as she let Nicole through a gate in the counter to the dining area on the other side. "That's just a little saying we have to remind us there's always something to do, even when we aren't serving food."

"Catchy."

"Mr. Roarke likes sayings that rhyme," Gail said, wrinkling her nose in a too-cute smile.

No kidding.

"The dining room will be your first station," Gail continued. "Everyone starts out here. Now, when you work in the dining room, you have a lot of things to do."

"I think I can handle it." Everyone paid for and picked up their food at the counter, just as

49

in any fast-food restaurant. Nicole couldn't imagine that carrying a few trays back to the counter could keep her very busy, even if she had to wash them or something.

"The person in the dining room is responsible for every aspect of its cleanliness. That means tables, floors, walls, windows, and ceiling."

"Ceiling?"

Gail grimaced. "Sometimes little kids play with the ketchup dispensers. Which reminds me, you also need to make sure that every table is fully stocked at all times."

She walked to the nearest one and gestured to the brightly colored plastic dispensers arrayed neatly along one edge. "You've got ketchup, mustard, relish, onions, and napkins. If any of those things are low, you replace them with full ones off the backup tray, then take the empties into the kitchen and fill them up. Except that they're never actually *empty*," Gail corrected herself quickly. "Never let anything run out. An empty dispenser makes Mr. Roarke crazy. He says it's a sign of poor planning."

"Don't we have a rhyme about that?" Nicole asked sarcastically.

"Attention to details means more sales," Gail spouted happily. "Thanks for reminding me."

"I was thinking more like, empty dispensers must be censored."

50

Gail's blue eyes went wide. "Oooh! Good one! You'll have to tell that to Mr. Roarke."

"Tell me what?" the restaurant manager asked, emerging from a short hall off the dining room. He was still in his twenties, Nicole guessed, or maybe early thirties. Too young to insist on being called Mister, in any event, but that was another unbreakable rule.

"Nothing," Nicole said quickly.

But Gail couldn't keep quiet. "Empty dispensers must be censored," she repeated in a sickeningly sweet tone of voice. "Isn't that good?"

Her cousin treated Mr. Roarke like a god. All Nicole could think about, though, was the fact that he barely came up to her shoulder—and that was despite his platform shoes. His hair was mouse brown and thinning, to go with his wimpy mustache.

He smiled, showing tiny teeth. "Ah, very clever. I'm glad to see you have the Wienerageous spirit. I knew I couldn't go wrong with any relative of Gail's."

"Oh, Mr. Roarke," Gail protested with a truly nauseating giggle.

"I hate to interrupt your training session," he continued. "But no one has done the quarterly bathroom check."

Gail looked horrified. "We'll get on that right away! Come on, Nicole."

Nicole wasn't sorry to have Gail lead her away

from the boss and down the hall he'd just come out of—until she learned the reason why.

"Whoever is working the dining room has to check the bathrooms every fifteen minutes," Gail said as the women's rest room door swung closed behind them. "We have a ten-point cleanliness guarantee posted here on the wall, but we employees just use it as a checklist."

Nicole scanned the list as Gail bustled around the stalls.

"We have to clean the *toilets*?" Nicole exclaimed, outraged.

Gail emerged from a stall holding a half-unwrapped roll of toilet paper. "They don't clean themselves. But you don't have to do it every quarter. Every hour is usually enough, unless someone gets sick or something."

She disappeared temporarily to put the paper on the roller, then popped the lid off the trash can by the sink and pulled out a big bag of used paper towels. "Come on. I'll show you where to get new garbage bags. We have to change the ones in the dining room, too, so we might as well do them all at once."

Nicole followed Gail into the hall.

"Duck in there and get the men's trash, would you?" Gail asked. "My hands are full."

"You don't expect me to go into the men's room!"

"It's no big deal. Everybody does it. Just knock on the door first and make sure no one's in there."

Nicole raised a hand to knock, then turned desperately back to Gail. "Couldn't I just work a cash register?"

Gail laughed as if she'd never heard a better joke. "Sure. Absolutely. When you get about six months' seniority, I'll be happy to teach you register. In the meantime—"

"Hey, Gail!" a guy's voice called from behind the counter. "Are you almost done with that trainee? We need a hand back here."

"I'll go!" Nicole volunteered immediately, desperate to get out of cleaning the bathrooms. Nothing happening in the kitchen could be worse than scrubbing toilets.

Not waiting for Gail's permission, Nicole ran to the dining room and let herself behind the counter, where two registers sat on the orange Formica. A third one lurked by the drive-through window. Behind them the soda dispensers and milk shake machines formed part of a head-high pass-through wall of stainless steel that divided the grills and fryers from the customers. Nicole flashed the two girls working the counter a weak smile before she scuttled around the corner, into the heart of the Wienerageous operation.

"There you are," the pimply guy she'd met before

said. She strained her memory and decided his name was Ajax.

The other cook in the kitchen waved a spatula in greeting. He wasn't bad-looking, but before Nicole had a chance to check him out, Ajax pointed to a corner of the bare concrete floor.

"Eric mopped and now we've got water all over the place."

Nicole looked blankly from the dingy gray puddle back to Ajax, not sure what he expected her to do about it.

"It's the grease," he explained. "It's clogged."

"Uh-huh." She still had no idea what he was talking about.

Ajax wiped his hands on his dirty red apron and smiled incredulously. "Don't tell me you've never cleaned a floor drain!"

Walking to the puddle, he reached down into its center and brought up a handful of dripping black goo.

"There's more where that came from," he promised. "Go get a bucket and brush from the back."

Four

Jenna spied from the front window as Caitlin and Abby disappeared down the street, Caitlin's head bent against the snow flurries that swirled through the bare trees. It was early, barely light outside, and Jenna wasn't due at the breakfast table for another half hour. The moment she was sure Caitlin wasn't going to turn back, she ran up the two flights of stairs to their bedroom and grabbed the telephone.

Mary Beth sounded half comatose when she picked up the call in Nashville. "Hullo?"

For a moment, Jenna almost chickened out. Her finger moved toward the disconnect button. But she was absolutely desperate to make things right with Caitlin, and that meant she had to know what was going on.

"Hi, Mary Beth. It's me. Jenna."

"Jenna? What's happening? Is something wrong?"

"Of course not," she said, with all the false cheer she could muster. "Why would anything be wrong?"

"Gee, I don't know," Mary Beth returned sarcastically. "Maybe because it's the crack of dawn and you're calling me now for the first time in your life."

"That's not true," Jenna protested, although she couldn't actually think of another time she had called Mary Beth at college. "And anyway, I thought you'd be up. Don't you have to go to class?"

"This is *college*, Jenna. Anyone who has half a clue how to work things here never has to be anywhere before ten o'clock."

"Is that true?"

"If you get real good, you take Tuesdays and Thursdays off too." A rustling came over the line as Mary Beth struggled to sit up in bed. "So what's going on, anyway? What's this all about?"

"I don't know," Jenna fibbed. "I just kind of miss you. I got so used to seeing you over the vacation that it seems weird not having you here anymore." In reality, Mary Beth had driven Jenna crazy during winter break by lounging around like the queen of the world while everyone else—especially Jenna—had to carry on with her chores. "Is it weird being back at school?"

"Uh, not really. I kind of live here now, you know."

"I thought maybe you missed your friends."

"I have more friends in Nashville than I do in Clearwater Crossing. I miss my friends when I'm *there*."

She wasn't making things easy, but Jenna pressed ahead. "It's just that after you spent so much time with all your high-school friends when you were here, I thought—"

"There's nothing else to do there, Jenna," Mary Beth said impatiently. "Does this conversation have a point?"

"Well, at least you *have* friends here. Caitlin's done nothing but work since she went to that New Year's Eve party with you and David Altmann." It wasn't as subtle as Jenna would have liked, but she had to bring up his name *somehow*. "It's kind of weird seeing David now, don't you think? He looks like Peter, only all grown up."

"I guess. I haven't spent a lot of time thinking about it."

"No?" That seemed like a good sign. Jenna took a deep breath. "Have you heard from him since you went back to school?"

"Why would I?"

"I don't know. I thought he mentioned writing you a letter."

"A letter? What about?"

"I don't know."

"Why?" Mary Beth asked with growing interest. "Does he have a crush on me or something?"

"No," Jenna said quickly. "I mean, uh, not that I'm aware of."

"Well, I don't know why he'd write to me, then."

Me either, Jenna thought, wishing she and her

oldest sister hadn't come to the same conclusion. "It was probably nothing. I must have misunderstood."

Mary Beth thought for a moment, then seemed to shrug it off. "So, how is Caitlin?" she asked. "Still working for that vet?"

"Of course. And she's walking dogs like crazy now. She's getting a ton of new clients in this cold weather."

They talked a few more minutes, discussing all the other members of their family. Jenna was glad that she'd successfully negotiated the most dangerous part of the call, but now that she had she was in a hurry to get off the phone.

"Well, I'd better go," she said. "I've got to get down to breakfast, and I guess you're going back to bed. Lucky!"

Mary Beth laughed. "All right. Say hi to everyone for me."

"Sure."

But as Jenna hung up the phone she knew that was one message she'd never pass along. The last thing she needed was for Caitlin to find out she'd called Mary Beth.

Except that she probably will. Sooner or later Mary Beth would be home for a visit and the topic would come up. Jenna could only imagine what Caitlin's reaction to that news would be.

And what if Mary Beth started thinking about David and decided to give *him* a call now?

"What an idiot I am!" Jenna moaned, falling backward onto her bed.

Until she had called her, Mary Beth had been totally clueless about David's interest. But now that Jenna had opened that door, was there any chance her sister would follow up?

The possibility made her queasy.

And what's the story with David anyway? I can't believe he put Caitlin through all that trauma and then never even wrote to Mary Beth.

"Jenna!" Mrs. Conrad called from downstairs. "Let's get going."

"Coming!" Jenna called back, not moving a muscle.

When was she going to learn that every time she meddled in Caitlin's life she only made things worse?

Okay, this time I'm serious, Nicole thought, spotting Courtney as her friend joined the long line to buy a cafeteria lunch.

For the last couple of days, ever since Nicole had returned home from Los Angeles, Courtney had ignored her—which was to say she'd made a huge point of letting Nicole know she was being ignored. Nicole had been so wrapped up in her other problems that she hadn't had the energy to break Courtney's ice, but that day she was determined to try.

It shouldn't be too hard to say I'm sorry about what happened, because I really, really am.

Even more so now that her dream trip had ended

in the nightmare of working at Wienerageous. Nicole hated everybody there, and she hated her family more for making her take the job. Her parents got most of the blame, of course, but it wasn't as if Heather was so innocent. Her stupid TP'ing plan was the reason Nicole had been busted in the first place. But instead of lying low, or showing even a speck of normal human sympathy, Heather was having a field day with Nicole's new occupation.

"Should you be putting that thing in *there*?" she'd asked smirkingly the night before as Nicole had stuffed her uniform into the washer. "I hope all that grease doesn't clog the drain." This morning it had been, "Wow! Look at that pimple! Well, don't feel bad, Nicole. You'll probably get tons of them now— but people will understand, don't you think?"

Nicole would have throttled her for sure if her parents hadn't been sitting right there. Instead she'd had to settle for giving everyone dirty looks and stalking out of the dining room, leaving for school without so much as a good-bye. Not that she was exchanging excess conversation with her parents lately anyway, and the way her sister had been behaving, Nicole didn't care if she never talked to Heather again.

She did want to talk to Courtney, though. . . .

Taking a deep breath, Nicole adjusted the backpack hanging off her shoulder, then squeezed the pocket in front to make sure the gift she'd bought was still there. Reassured, she snuck up behind her friend, trying to act as if Courtney had been saving her place all along to avoid a confrontation with the other people in line.

"I hear they serve an excellent mystery meat here," she said, hoping for a smile.

Courtney turned around slowly, her green eyes like chips off a glacier. "That's the best you can do?"

"No. Uh . . . uh . . . I brought you a present from Hollywood."

Courtney's lips pursed tightly. For a moment Nicole was afraid she'd be sorry for even alluding to the fact that the country *had* a west coast.

"What did you bring me?" she asked at last, curiosity winning out.

Nicole's backpack was off her shoulder in a flash. Balancing it across her knee, she unzipped the front pocket and took out a crumpled paper bag.

"I would have wrapped it," she said nervously, "but I thought the bag was kind of cool. I mean, it says 'Hollywood' and everything."

Courtney glanced up the line ahead of them, to gauge how much longer they'd wait for their turn, then took the bag and opened it. Reaching into the tissue paper, she pulled out a silver sand dollar suspended by a light chain.

"I never even got to the beach," Nicole admitted as Courtney examined the necklace. "I guess they have sand dollars there. I mostly stayed in the hotel."

61

Courtney glanced up. "That doesn't sound very fun."

"It wasn't. I had a lousy time, actually. I never should have gone without you."

Courtney tossed her red hair, as if to say that much was obvious.

"Are we eating or what?" a guy behind them in line demanded. "Quit yakking and get a tray."

Courtney shot him a lethal glance, then picked up a tray anyhow.

Both girls took the pizza and salad, although Nicole went for a diet soda while Courtney added a big hunk of berry pie to her tray. Courtney was silent as they paid for their lunches, and Nicole's anxiety rose by the second. Had they made up or not? She fidgeted as they exited the line and stood at the edge of the crowded main room.

"Where do you want to sit?" Courtney asked, surveying the possibilities.

Court's going to sit with me! If she wasn't completely forgiven, she had to be on the way.

"Over there looks pretty good." Nicole nodded toward a group of sparsely populated tables on the other side of the room. She and Courtney began to walk.

"So are your parents letting you have the car tonight, or do you need a ride?" Courtney asked.

"Tonight?" Nicole echoed distractedly, zeroing in on her table of choice.

"For the basketball game. If you want, I can pick you up."

Nicole's feet kept moving toward the table, but for a moment everything else seemed to stop: time, her heart, her breathing. . . .

She'd forgotten about the away game that night, and with the tip-off at seven and her shift not ending until seven-thirty, she couldn't possibly make it. She'd have to change out of her uniform before she went home—there was no way she was venturing out in public in that clown suit—then shower and change again before she could go to the game. She had already learned that the air inside Wienerageous had a smell all its own, one that clung like a vile perfume to everyone who worked there.

"Well, I, um . . . I think I'm busy," Nicole stammered in a panic. She couldn't tell Courtney about Wienerageous. Not Courtney. "I'm, uh, helping my mom with . . . some stuff."

Courtney looked at her as if she had grown two heads. "You expect me to believe that?"

They had reached the chosen table. Nicole put down her tray, but Courtney held on to hers.

"Look, Court," Nicole pleaded. "I didn't know you were going to invite me to the game. Is it my fault I have other plans?"

"Ha! So now you *admit* you have other plans! Why don't you just tell the truth, Nicole?"

"You make it sound like I'm purposely doing something without you," Nicole whined. "And that isn't—"

"Just . . . have a nice lunch," Courtney cut her off scornfully. Her eyes were icy again and her lip curled with sarcasm. "Better still, have a nice life."

Spinning on her heel, she stalked off toward the friends she'd been eating with the last couple of days.

"Court!" Nicole called after her, but though several heads turned, none of them was Courtney's.

"Great," Nicole muttered, sinking onto the empty bench in front of her. "Just perfect."

She and Courtney had been so close to making up. . . .

Now everything was ruined.

I hate that stupid job, she thought. *The second that vase is paid off, I'll never set foot in that grease pit again!*

Melanie took her time walking by the cafeteria table where Jesse and his football friends were sitting. The cheerleaders were wearing their skirts and sweaters that day in honor of the evening's basketball game—and Melanie would have had to be blind not to have noticed that Jesse had always liked her in that outfit. She could hear conversations fall off along the length of the room as she passed by, but she put a little extra attitude into her step anyway, just to make her point.

Tanya Jeffries and Angela Maldonado were laughing when Melanie joined their table.

"That was quite a walk," Tanya teased as Melanie sat beside her. "Were you trying for someone in particular, or just reminding the whole school that you're still around?"

Melanie tossed her head. "Maybe a little of both."

Attracting attention was something she rarely did on purpose, but it didn't hurt to remind Jesse how easily she did it—or that plenty of guys would love to be in his place. Pushing her tray forward to make room, she turned in her seat to see if he was looking.

He was. Their eyes met with a jolt, and for a moment she felt like she could almost read his soul. The old hunger shone forth, as deep and sharp-edged as before.

Then Jesse snorted and turned his head.

Melanie's heart pounded; her cheeks heated with embarrassment. Did the entire cafeteria know that scornful look had been for her?

"Well, what's the verdict?" Angela asked. "Did the right person notice?"

Melanie drew a deep, calming breath. If Angela hadn't seen it, it couldn't have been that obvious.

"He noticed," Melanie said. "And I think I added a couple of backups to my list."

"Who are you working on?" Tanya asked, her dark eyes full of mischief. "If you tell me, I might leave him alone so you'll have a chance."

Melanie laughed. "I could say the same thing to you, but I don't hear you volunteering any names."

"Yeah, Tanya," said Angela, distracted. "Who is it?"

Tanya had been hinting around since New Year's Eve that she had a crush on someone, but she'd steadfastly refused to say who. Melanie was starting to wonder if there was really a guy involved, or if Tanya was simply enjoying driving them crazy guessing.

"I'll let you know when I seal the deal," Tanya promised. "Right now, that's for me to know and him to find out."

"Yeah, yeah." Angela rolled her eyes. "You'd better *hope* we don't find out at this point."

The two friends continued trading gibes, giving Melanie the opportunity to risk another peek back over her shoulder at Jesse.

He had twisted around on the bench so that she could no longer see his profile. Instead, his back faced her squarely, broad and strong beneath his green letterman's jacket. The nonverbal message was clear: He didn't want anything to do with her.

Except that he did. She'd just seen it in his eyes. So why was he acting like a split personality?

Because you hurt his pride.

Breaking things off with Jesse had been the kind of kick in the ego he wasn't used to. And with an ego as big as Jesse's, should she be surprised if it took him a while to recover?

He still likes me, Melanie reassured herself, facing her friends again. *If he didn't, would he be such a pain in the butt?*

Even so, there was only so much abuse a girl could take. Melanie began eating lunch, wondering what she ought to do next.

I'll give him a couple of days, she decided. *Maybe if I ignore him, he'll come to his senses.*

She nodded, happy with her plan. She was patient—she could wait.

By the next time I look Jesse's way, he'll be dying to talk to me.

Five

"I hope you're not going to spend all day studying, *mi vida*," Mrs. del Rios said worriedly, walking into the kitchen. "You're working too hard lately."

Miguel shrugged without lifting his eyes from the math text on the table. "We need the money."

"Yes, but we don't need *you* to make it all. Besides, it's Saturday. Why don't you go to the movies with Leah? Do something fun for a change."

"I have to get caught up. We're having a test on Monday and I've barely even looked at this stuff."

Mrs. del Rios pulled on her coat. "Suit yourself, but if you don't watch out you may wake up one morning and discover you don't have a girlfriend."

Miguel's head jerked up from his papers. "What's that supposed to mean?" He had gone to a lot of trouble to make sure his mother had no idea of his current troubles with Leah. "What makes you say that?"

Mrs. del Rios only smiled. "She's young, she's beautiful, and by now she's getting bored. I was seventeen once—it's not that hard to remember."

"Oh," he said, relieved. His mother didn't know anything after all. "Are you going to be busy at the store today?"

"I doubt it. I think the Christmas returns are over, and so is our sale. It ought to be a nice, quiet day."

"Good."

Miguel was grateful that his mother's kidney transplant had allowed her to resume a normal life, including returning full-time to the department store sales job she'd held before she'd become so ill, but he still worried about her getting too tired. He'd liked it better when she'd done secretarial work at their church office, but that had only been part-time and hadn't paid nearly enough to live on.

"I'll see you tonight," his mother said, moving toward the kitchen door. "But if I come home and find a note that says you went out instead, that would be even better."

"You don't *want* me to pass this math test?"

"Of course I do. But if you put in three or four hours today and the same amount tomorrow, that ought to be plenty. You don't have to devote your entire weekend to it."

A car horn sounded outside.

"Oops. There's my ride. At least think it over, *mi hijo*."

After she had gone, Miguel tried to concentrate again, but it was no use. Pushing the book away, he

69

got up and walked to the living room window. Outside, a thin layer of snow coated the ground, and the sky looked inclined to drop more. The weather hadn't stopped Rosa from taking off with her friends, though, leaving him alone.

Miguel sighed. There really wasn't any reason he couldn't go out too. He did have a lot of studying to do, but if he buckled down and got serious he could finish it all exactly the way his mother had said. But how could he call Leah for a date now, when everything was so up in the air between them?

He couldn't.

On the other hand, how could he go out and *not* call Leah?

He couldn't.

If Leah ever found out I went anywhere after that sob story I gave her about needing to study, I'd be in serious trouble.

He rubbed his aching temples. *I mean in more serious trouble.*

And it was pretty hard to imagine being in a worse predicament than he was already in. Sinking down onto the couch, Miguel hooked his chin over its padded back and stared unseeingly through the window.

He never could have guessed things would turn around the way they had.

When he had proposed to Leah, he had meant it

with all his heart. But now that she had surprised him by saying she was considering his offer, Miguel was the one suddenly thinking of reasons that getting married might not be a good idea.

Wouldn't Leah just end up hating him if she sacrificed her college dreams? But if she didn't, how would they get by?

There was an even bigger problem, though, and she had just walked out the door. His mother would be devastated if her only son wasn't married in the Catholic church, and that wasn't a possibility unless Leah agreed to convert and to raise their children Catholic. Miguel knew Leah's mind was still open on the subject of God, but he didn't think she'd be willing to convert. *Knowing Leah, she'd probably see that as closing her mind.*

And there was more. When his mother had been so sick, in need of a transplant it seemed she would never get, Miguel had made a desperate promise to God. *Make my mother well*, he'd begged, *and I'll never doubt you again*.

Not long after that, Mrs. del Rios had received her new kidney and, to make good on his vow, Miguel had begun attending mass for the first time since his father's death. If he were to leave his church to get married in some other ceremony, would that be going back on his promise? Or did God even care about things like denominations?

71

I don't know about God, but I know someone who cares a lot, he thought, focusing on the bootprints his mother had left in the snow.

Could he really break her heart like that?

Mr. Roarke pointed at his watch.

"There are two minutes left in your shift, Nicole. Here at Wienerageous, we don't pay people to stand around. Go wipe down those dining room tables and then you can clock out."

"But, Mr. Roarke . . ."

There was no way anyone could wipe all those tables in two minutes, but one look into her boss's small eyes and Nicole shut up on the spot. He was really kind of creepy, she'd decided. Definitely not someone she wanted to mess with. Grabbing a wet towel, she left the counter, where she'd been chatting with a cashier named Ann about her plans for the rest of that Saturday, and flounced into the dining room.

I hate that guy. He's such a dweeb, she thought as she cleaned the tables.

She would have liked to throw her stinky wet towel into her boss's self-satisfied face, but she barely dared to think it. *Not that I'd do it anyway, but with Mom and Dad so hot on me having this stupid job, if I get in trouble here I'm dead at home.*

Forget that without a paycheck she'd never be able to pay for that crystal vase. What was worse was that the unflattering comparisons with Gail, Miss Star Employee, would never end. Speaking of whom . . .

"Wow, the shift's over and you're still at it," Gail said admiringly, emerging from the hall that led to the bathrooms. "Mr. Roarke is going to love to see that."

Nicole forced a smile that was more like a grimace and pushed a limp strand of hair back under her hat. Although Gail held a mop in one hand and a bucket in the other, her uniform was almost as fresh as when she'd come in that morning. No one looking at the two of them would ever guess that she and Nicole had just finished the same ten-to-two shift, including a lunch rush that put the weekday traffic to shame. Nicole's face was slick with the grease she'd inhaled, her tunic was blotched with ketchup and mustard, and a huge splat of relish had dried on top of one of her shoes, curling at the edges like some bizarre species of seaweed.

"I feel guilty knocking off while you're still working," Gail said, "but I guess I'll see you in the break room in a minute?"

"In *less* than a minute," Nicole returned through clenched teeth.

Gail flashed her a dazzling smile. Her skin didn't have a trace of shine anywhere, and her hair looked freshly combed. "Knock and I'll let you in," she said before she disappeared with her bucket.

Great, Nicole thought, wiping another table. It wasn't bad enough she had to work every shift with Gail—she had to change clothes with her too.

By the time Nicole finished Mr. Roarke's last-minute assignment and knocked for Gail to let her into the break room, her cousin had already changed into a cabled sweater beneath a pair of black overalls. She had brushed her hair into a ponytail, which she held with one hand while she opened the door with the other.

"There you are!" she greeted Nicole. "I was starting to think you'd already left."

"Wearing this circus tent?" Nicole couldn't keep the scorn out of her voice. "If there were elephants in this town, they'd probably follow me home."

Gail actually smiled a little. "Listen, could you do me a favor? There's a scrunchie in my backpack, and I should have gotten it out before I got my hair all fixed, but . . . could you get it for me?" She pointed to her backpack with her free hand while her other held on to her hair.

Why not? Nicole thought irritably, as she yanked the zipper open. *I do everyone else's grunt work around here*. The scrunchie was pink and right on top. *Maybe after this I could polish her shoes or—*

Oh, my God.

Nicole froze with the pink band in her hand, her disbelieving eyes glued to the item that had lain beneath it. A half-empty packet of cigarettes spilled its contents through the torn foil at the top, scattering them into the pouch.

She's holding them for someone. She must be, Nicole thought, her heart still racing with the shock. It was inconceivable that a career brownnoser like her cousin actually smoked. Nicole didn't smoke, and she was way wilder than Gail. Tearing her eyes from the incriminating evidence in the backpack, she handed Gail the scrunchie.

"Thanks." Gail began winding it through her hair as if she had no idea what Nicole had just seen.

She probably doesn't, Nicole realized. *She's been holding those smokes for someone so long, she's forgotten they're in there.*

It was hard to believe that Gail would bend the rules even as far as that, but Nicole was certain that was the explanation. If those were really Gail's cigarettes, she would never have risked having Nicole look into her backpack—what if Nicole told Aunt Ellen?

"Well, I guess I'm ready," Gail said, letting go of her perfect ponytail. "If you're going to change clothes, Nicole, you ought to hurry. The guys are going to want to get in here soon."

"Huh? Oh."

She had totally forgotten that that was what she'd come in there to do. She moved toward her things in a daze as Gail grabbed her backpack and headed for the door.

"You, uh . . . you might want to zip that up," Nicole said to her cousin's back. "You don't want your cigarettes spilling out."

Gail stopped walking immediately. But instead of denying the cigarettes were hers, she simply zipped up the pocket.

"Thanks. I don't need Roarke spotting them, either. Okay. See you on Monday," she said, reaching for the doorknob.

They *were* hers, then!

"You shouldn't smoke," Nicole blurted out, like a total mama's girl.

Gail just smiled roguishly. "Don't you ever do anything you're not supposed to?"

She was gone before Nicole could gather her wits to reply. What else did Gail do that she wasn't supposed to?

Six

"Sarah, stop dawdling and eat your waffles," Mrs. Conrad said. "You don't want to be late for church."

With the exception of Mary Beth, the entire Conrad family was sitting around the dining room table in its familiar Sunday-morning routine. Jenna glanced at the wall clock and began eating a little faster.

"I could always go to the second service with Caitlin," Sarah said, dragging the back of her fork through the syrup on her plate.

"What?" Mrs. Conrad looked from Sarah to Caitlin. "You're not coming to church with us?"

"I need to walk a few more dogs this morning," Caitlin said, her voice barely above a whisper. "I thought I could finish them all before breakfast, but this ice is slowing me down."

"How many dogs are you walking these days?" Mr. Conrad asked. "You were gone before I even got up this morning."

"Too many," Mrs. Conrad said decisively.

"Not really," Caitlin said. "It's just this weather."

"You already have a full-time job with Dr. Campbell," her mother said. "I don't know why you need to walk dogs, but if you have to, I think you either need fewer dogs or more help."

"*More* help?" Maggie jumped in. "How about *some* help?"

Allison looked up from her sausage. "Maybe you could hire someone, Caitlin, and have your own business. You could call it Cat and Dogs."

Jenna smiled, and not only at the rare burst of originality from Allison. Here was her chance to show Caitlin how sorry she was, like Peter had suggested!

"I'll help!" she volunteered. "I'll help for free."

"That's all right," Caitlin declined quickly. "Mom needs you in the choir."

Jenna sang in their church choir every Sunday, but this was such a golden opportunity . . .

"Could you get by without me, Mom?" Jenna asked her choir director. "Just this once? Just for the early service?"

Mrs. Conrad looked back and forth between her two daughters. "I suppose. At least that way I know Caitlin will finish up in time. I don't like it, though—and I definitely don't want this to happen again next Sunday. You'll have to plan better, Caitlin."

"I can help you next week too," Jenna said. "I'll get up really early so we can finish before church."

"That's quite an offer, Jenna," their father said jovially. "It looks to me like you've got a partner, Caitlin."

Any of her other sisters would have turned her down—and told her off—right there, but Jenna was counting on Caitlin not to want a scene that might divulge her secret.

"I'll meet you in the garage," Caitlin said, pushing back her chair. "You'd better change your clothes," she added with a glance at Jenna's church outfit.

Jenna wolfed down the last two bites of her waffle and hurried to change and join her sister.

Outside, most of the snow had melted, refreezing overnight into a slippery layer of ice. Caitlin took off the moment Jenna appeared, striding down the icy driveway at a pace that left Jenna slip-sliding in all directions. Not daring to complain, she did her best to get her legs beneath her and keep pace with her taller sister. It wasn't until they had picked up all four of the dogs they were supposed to walk that Jenna found the courage to speak.

"If I'm supposed to be helping you, you ought to at least let me take one of those leashes."

"I don't need your help," Caitlin said, struggling to maintain her footing with all four dogs pulling in different directions.

"I changed my clothes, I'm out here freezing my butt off, I'm missing church . . . and I'm walking one of those dogs." Jenna grabbed the leash of a large, caramel brown mutt named Rex and tried to pull it from her sister's mittened hand. "Let go."

Caitlin shot her an irritated look, then handed over the dog. "If he lands you flat on your back, don't come crying to me."

"I think I can handle him."

But hanging on to Rex definitely made walking on ice a lot harder—and the dog seemed to realize she was a novice. Whereas he had walked reasonably sedately with Caitlin, now he strained at the end of the leash, his breath billowing like a steam engine.

"Stop it, Rex," Jenna scolded, pulling back on the leash. Rex scrabbled wildly on the icy path, his toenails throwing a shower of slush onto Jenna's jeans. "Whoa!"

"Give him back if he's too much for you."

"I can handle him," Jenna repeated stubbornly, doing her best to prove it. She'd look like a total idiot if she had to admit defeat now. Especially since Caitlin was still walking three dogs and she had only one.

They came to a dead end, and Caitlin struck off across a field. The thin layer of snow was still relatively undisturbed there, except where passersby had crunched it flat into dirty gray pathways. Random sets of paw prints indicated that Caitlin's dogs weren't the first ones to happen along. In the middle of the field she bent and began unhooking leashes.

"You can let Rex off now too. This is a good place for them to run."

Gladly! Jenna thought, reaching down to comply.

Rex took off like a shot, racing straight through the field toward a line of bare trees in the distance.

"Is he coming back?" she asked worriedly. She had visions of tracking that beast through the slush for hours, missing church, and lunch, and dinner . . .

"He'll be back," Caitlin said confidently. "If he doesn't show up when I whistle, he knows he won't get his treat." She pulled a plastic bag of dog biscuits out of her parka pocket and held them up for Jenna to see. "Works like a charm."

Jenna relaxed a little as she stood watching the other three dogs with Caitlin. They crashed around in the snow a little, but mostly they sniffed everything in sight, zigzagging back and forth until the field looked like a giant doodle pad.

In her mind, Jenna rehearsed a hundred things to say. She wanted desperately to tell Caitlin that David had never written to Mary Beth, that Mary Beth didn't even seem that interested. But how could she without revealing her continued snooping? If Caitlin found out about that phone call, Jenna was sure to be even worse off than before.

I shouldn't have involved Mary Beth, she thought with a silent moan. She'd promised herself she was going to stay out of Caitlin's business. Not to mention the promise she'd made to Caitlin . . .

Jenna peeked timidly at her sister's profile, but Caitlin ignored her, as she'd been doing all week.

I could be singing in church right now for all the good this is doing me. At least people there give me the time of day. She wriggled her toes inside their wet shoes. *And I wouldn't be freezing, either.*

"Caitlin, what do I have to do to make you forgive me?" she burst out, frustrated.

Caitlin sighed and finally turned her head. "It's not that easy, Jenna. It's more a question of what you would have to *undo*."

But her voice was a little less distant, and her eyes had softened, too. Jenna's heart pumped faster.

Was she wearing her sister down?

Melanie was sitting at the breakfast bar when her father shuffled past her into the kitchen, his eyes glassy and unfocused. His threadbare robe was tied crookedly around his shrunken frame, and he rubbed his silver-stubbled chin as he made his way to the refrigerator.

"Hard night, Dad?" Melanie asked sarcastically, watching him gulp orange juice from the carton. Pushing the remnants of her pastry out of the way, she gave her father her full attention.

Mr. Andrews finished the juice before he answered. "I'm fine."

"Or you will be when you get a few beers in on top of that," she sneered, too bitter to hide her feelings.

She had suspected that he was still drinking, despite his Christmas Eve promise to quit, but in the last few days moderation had gone out the window, along with any attempt to hide what he was doing. Melanie had desperately wanted to believe that he was turning over a new leaf, that her pleas had finally gotten through to him, but she should have known better. Her father's first love was his dead wife; his second had become the alcohol-induced numbness he cultivated in her memory.

"So much for rehab, huh?"

Mr. Andrews shrugged impatiently. "I don't need to go to rehab when I can do the same thing right here for free. I don't even need to quit, really. It's not like drinking is preventing me from working or anything."

"That's because you don't work, Dad! You *promised* me—"

"I promised I'd try to cut back. And I'm trying."

"You're not trying very hard."

He shook his head, then quickly put a hand to it, as if to still its rattling contents. "What do you know about hard? I'm not going to talk about this, Melanie."

Grabbing a soda, he slammed the refrigerator and walked back out the way he'd come in. A moment later, the den door closed behind him.

Melanie dropped her head onto the counter. The cold tile pressed her cheekbone uncomfortably, but instead of sitting up again she welcomed the distraction. She leaned into the counter harder, trying to turn her discomfort to pain.

You're an idiot if any of this surprises you, she told herself. *When are you going to learn?*

But even though her father's behavior was exactly what she had expected, she was still desperately disappointed. Tears ran down onto the tile, filling the space between the ceramic and her cheek. She slid her face back and forth on the slippery surface, rocking the pain away.

I can't do this, she thought. *Not again*.

She had actually started to believe she was through the worst of the tragedy that had devastated her family. But if her father was opting out of her life again . . .

The prospect of being alone made her thoughts return to Jesse. Did she really care about him, or was he just a way of filling the emptiness she felt?

Lifting her head from the counter, she wiped her wet face with both hands.

Someone has to fill it.

Miguel and his family were on the steps outside All Souls Church, on their way home after mass, when he spotted Sabrina walking ahead of them to the curb. Her dark hair swung loose down the back of her coat, mingling with the fringe of a lavender scarf.

"There's Sabrina," he said, pointing. "Do you think she came alone?"

"Sabrina!" Mrs. del Rios called delightedly.

Sabrina turned, then waved and waited for them

84

to join her. Her cheeks were already flushed with the cold, matching the pink of her lips.

"You look so pretty, dear," Mrs. del Rios said. "Where are your parents?"

Sabrina flashed a bright smile. "Everyone else went to mass last night, but I had a date, so here I am."

Miguel was kind of curious to know who she'd gone out with, but before he could ask her, Rosa changed the subject.

"Hey, Sabrina," she piped up. "Was Sister Eugenia at Sacred Heart when you were there?"

"Sister Eugenia was there when my *mother* was there," Sabrina answered, laughing. "She must be at least ninety."

"Do you happen to have the paper you wrote for her on the American Revolution? Everyone says it's impossible to get a good grade on that one, so I need all the help I can get."

"Rosa!" Mrs. del Rios scolded, with a nervous backward glance a the church. Father Sebastian was still standing outside the main door, chatting with people as they exited. "You are *not* going to copy Sabrina's paper," she said, in a slightly lower voice.

"You don't *want* to copy my paper," Sabrina told her, still chuckling. "Believe me."

With a roll of her eyes, she turned to Miguel. "You're awfully quiet this morning. What's the problem? Still asleep?"

Before Miguel could answer, Rosa jumped in again. "You're kidding, right? Mr. Talkative?"

"Maybe Miguel talks more at work," Mrs. del Rios said.

"Not really," Sabrina replied, with a conspirator's wink at Miguel. "That's one of his many virtues."

Mrs. del Rios pulled her good black coat tighter to her body. "Why don't you join us for lunch, Sabrina? We'd love to have you."

"I think Miguel has probably seen enough of me this week. . . ." Her eyes invited him to say so.

"Don't be silly," Mrs. del Rios said. "It's been too long since you've come to the house. Besides, I'm making enchiladas."

"Yeah, come on, Sabrina," Rosa told her. "You'd be crazy to pass up my mom's enchiladas."

"I know," Sabrina said, putting a hand to her flat stomach. "I remember."

Miguel was silent as they walked out to his car. Leah would probably have a fit about Sabrina coming to his house—if he were ever dumb enough to tell her—but there couldn't really be anything wrong with it. Sabrina was simply an old family friend. Besides, his mother had invited her.

Back at the house, Rosa stuck to Sabrina like glue, obviously a little in awe. From what Miguel could gather, Sabrina was something of a legend at Sacred Heart. And, of course, she was pretty good-looking too.

"You can sit here," Rosa said, pulling out her own dinette chair for Sabrina as the group walked into the kitchen.

The smell of slowly baking enchiladas filled the room, making Miguel's mouth water. Mrs. del Rios cracked the oven door open to check on them while Miguel went to the refrigerator for sodas and the salad he'd made that morning.

Sabrina hesitated beside the chair. "Is there something I can do to help you, Mrs. del Rios?"

"Aren't you sweet? No, you sit down, dear. We've got this under control."

Miguel put a glass on the table in front of her while Rosa went to get the plates and silverware. "It seems weird to see you and not be working," he said.

Sabrina raised one arched brow. "We've only been working together a couple of weeks. We used to see each other all the time before that."

"Not *all* the time, dear," Mrs. del Rios corrected, putting a dish of sour cream on the table Rosa was setting. "I haven't seen you in ages. How are your parents? Tell us about your brothers and sisters."

Sabrina smiled. "Everyone's fine. The siblings are all still in school, wishing they were out, and . . . Wow! Those look fantastic."

"They're only cheese," Mrs. del Rios said modestly, but her expression showed how pleased she was with Sabrina's review of her enchiladas.

After the food had been served and the blessing

said, Sabrina filled them in on the doings of her parents and brothers and sisters. It seemed she had an endless supply of funny stories about her younger siblings, not to mention her uncles, aunts, and cousins. Miguel watched her as he ate, focusing more on her face than her words.

Sabrina had always been charming. Even when they were kids she could wrap anybody's parents around her little finger. Maybe it was her smile, or her happy nature, or those astonishing amethyst eyes. Whatever it was, Sabrina was obviously working her magic again—this time on Rosa and his mother. They hung on her descriptions of her large and boisterous family, peppering her with questions each time she paused for a bite.

If Sabrina and I got married, Miguel thought, *what a blowout that would be*.

There was absolutely no doubt that their thrilled parents would insist on a wedding of epic proportions. The ceremony would be at All Souls, of course, and Sabrina would have about a million bridesmaids to include all those sisters and cousins. Miguel could see it all as clearly as if the wedding album were already open in front of him: He and Sabrina at the altar, Sabrina stunning in white lace and white flowers. The groomsmen would wear black tuxedos, like his, the bridesmaids violet dresses exactly the shade of Sabrina's eyes . . .

What am I thinking? he wondered with a start. *Am I crazy?*

He liked Sabrina, sure. He liked her a lot, in fact.

But I don't love Sabrina, he reminded himself. *I love Leah.*

So why was imagining a wedding with Sabrina so easy when every time he tried to see one with Leah he drew a total blank?

Seven

Has Miguel changed his mind?

Leah's heart shrank from the thought, but she couldn't seem to push it out of her head.

Looking up from the book she was pretending to read, she stared off into space across the back corner of the school library. It hadn't been so long ago that she and Miguel had hidden out in that corner together nearly every afternoon. But Miguel was at work again that Monday, and Leah was on her own.

If he doesn't want to get married, why doesn't he just say so?

In Los Angeles she had made up her mind to accept his proposal despite the obvious sacrifices doing so would entail. But now he seemed to want to back out.

What should I do? she wondered. *Confront him or forget the whole thing?* She sighed. *If I were smart, I'd be glad he wants to drop it.*

But she wasn't glad. Not at all.

It would be better if the idea of marriage had never

come up than to walk away from it like this, without even understanding why.

Rising abruptly from the table, Leah gathered her books and began stuffing them into her pack. A moment later she strode out the library door. She paid no attention to the fact that the sun was finally out, rendering the weather almost pleasant, but instead hurried across the soggy lawn to the student parking lot.

Her mother had let her have her car that day, and as Leah reached the driver's door all she could think about was getting off on her own somewhere. Her parents were still at work; she could have the condo to herself. But she knew if she went home she'd only end up staring at the walls and worrying until her parents got there. Then, the moment they did, she'd retreat into her room, totally unable to talk to them about what was on her mind.

How could she? They'd freak out if they knew she was even considering marriage. And, in a way, that was the worst part of the whole thing.

I'll go to the lake, she decided. The roads were dry, and so what if she'd only sit in the car and stare out the window? At least at the lake she'd feel close to Miguel.

She missed him so much. If it hurt this badly just to have him working an afternoon job, she couldn't imagine how painful it would be if they ever broke up. Her gut ached to even think about losing him.

91

What is he doing right now? she wondered, turning the key in the ignition. *Is he thinking about me?*

Or was he thinking about Sabrina? Was he sorry he'd ever proposed? Because that was how it looked. There was no doubt in Leah's mind that something had changed since she'd left for L.A.

Why was he so hot on marrying me then when now he barely gives me the time of day?

A horrible thought occurred to her: Had Miguel changed his mind because she had lost the U.S. Girls contest? *Maybe he only wanted to marry me because he thought I would be some big model.*

The idea was completely revolting.

How could a marriage proposal—something that ought to make her feel so good—make her so completely miserable?

"Nicole!" Gail called from the front counter. "Can you come out here a minute?"

"Now what?" Nicole groaned. She had begged Ajax and Eric to let her help them in the kitchen because she hadn't wanted to get stuck working the dining room again, doing the quarterly bathroom checks, but she should have known better than to ask Ajax for a favor. He'd pounced on her offer immediately—then stood her at a cutting board in front of an entire bag of onions.

"Chop them fine," he'd admonished, handing her a butcher's knife. "Mr. Roarke hates chunks."

And I hate Mr. Roarke, she'd thought, but she hadn't dared to say anything of the kind.

Her eyes were half-swollen now, and she had a headache from all the onion-induced tears she'd sniffed back, but there weren't any chunks in the bin she was filling—she was absolutely certain of that.

"Ni-*cooooole!*"

"Yes. Yes, I'm coming."

Putting down the knife, she wiped the back of her pink-and-orange sleeve across her eyes and headed for the front.

"Hurry back," Ajax told her bossily. "If you're done with those onions, you can fill up the bun warmers."

"Absolutely, Ajax. I'm just *aching* to do your bidding."

Nicole heard Eric snicker as she walked away.

At the end of the pass-through wall, where she had to turn the corner to get to the counter, she almost collided with Mr. Roarke.

"You're on the clock, Nicole. Tell your friend we don't encourage this type of thing."

"What type of thing?" she asked, but Mr. Roarke was already walking away.

What friend? she added silently as she rounded the corner. Surely he didn't mean Gail?

"What do you want, Gail?" Nicole asked impatiently, walking up behind her cousin. "Mr. Roarke is totally tweaked off now and . . . what?"

The grin on Gail's face was verging on goofy. Instead of answering, she pointed out into the dining room, at a customer who looked a lot like—

"Guy!" Nicole gasped. "What are you doing here?"

Her horrified voice turned heads in the tiny restaurant. Guy stared at her as well, reminding her what she was wearing. Nicole felt the blush burning up to her cheeks, but there was nowhere she could run.

"Do you have ESP or something?" she whined. "How do you keep showing up in the worst imaginable places?"

The smile died on Guy Vaughn's face. "You don't sound happy to see me."

"Happy to see you? You've got to be . . . cripes!"

"Go talk to him outside," Gail whispered, elbowing Nicole in the back. "I'll cover for you."

"How are you going to cover for me? I'm supposed to be filling the bun warmers and you have to work the register."

"Just go. Let me take care of it."

Nicole hesitated a second longer, then rushed out from behind the counter and grabbed Guy by the elbow, hustling him through the front door into the weak sunshine outside. If Mr. Roarke saw her she knew she'd be in trouble, but it was a chance she had to take. Anything was better than staying in the restaurant, where she might be forced to inform Guy that her smile was contagious. She dragged him along the pavement to a hidden corner of the building, breathing hard from the combination of shock and embarrassment.

"What are you doing here?" she repeated, mortified.

"I came to see you." Guy turned his empty hands palm up. "Is that so wrong?"

"How did you know where to find me?"

She had gone to great lengths to make sure no one knew about her job. Not Courtney, not Eight Prime—no one. And if Nicole had been making a special list of people she *really* didn't want to find out, Guy Vaughn would have been at the top.

From their first horrendous blind date to the foolish way she'd spilled her guts to him in Los Angeles, every time Nicole dealt with Guy she ended up looking stupid. She glanced down at her Wienerageous uniform and winced. *And this time I already have such a huge head start . . .*

"Heather told Greg, and Greg told me. Look, if you don't want me around, I'll just go." He turned to leave.

Nicole's hand shot out to stop him. Her fingers sank into his jacket sleeve and found a grip on his forearm.

"No, don't. I'm sorry."

I'm sorry my monster of a little sister can't keep her big mouth shut! she added silently, making a mental note to wreak havoc when she got home. It figured that Heather would tell her Sunday-school teacher about

Nicole's secret—she told him every other embarrassing thing she could think of. Still, now that Guy had already seen her at her worst, Nicole didn't want him to go away mad.

"I mean, it's not that I don't want to see you," she said. "I just don't want to see you *here*."

"Is your boss going to be mad at you?"

"Probably. But it's not even that."

How could she explain? She massaged her temples, trying to think of an angle he'd understand.

"I like your hat," Guy said in the silence.

Was he *kidding*? Nicole jerked her hands away from her face.

Guy was smiling again. His mouth twitched at the corners, and even the reddish brown hair falling over his eyes couldn't hide how full of amusement they were. He *was* kidding!

"Guy!" she wailed. "This isn't funny!"

"Sorry."

For a moment he wrestled his face into something more serious. Then he burst out laughing. "I'm sorry, Nicole, but it kind of is. I mean, not that you have a job—that part's great. But that it's here. I mean, *you* . . . working *here* . . ."

"Yes. Yes, I get it," she said impatiently.

When I get home, Heather had better run for her life, she vowed.

Why had her parents let her sister go to Sunday

school anyway, when the little creep was supposed to be grounded? *Don't they know that Sunday school is her Disneyland?*

"Listen, Guy, could you do me a favor? Could you never tell anyone you saw me here? Ever?"

"It's not that bad, Nicole. The shoes are pretty normal, and the hat . . . okay, the hat is a problem," he admitted, still laughing. "But I'd *love* to get three for my band. Could you see us playing a school dance in those?"

"I'd pay a lot not to see it," she said sullenly. "Besides, you're too good to play school dances. You ought to make an album."

"You think so?" he asked earnestly.

She shrugged. "You can sing, Guy. I mean, you can *really* sing."

"Thanks."

"Yeah. Well, I'd better get back to work before my boss gives himself a hernia. I'll see you later."

"Actually, I was planning to come in and eat. I forgot to pack a lunch today and—"

"Oh, you don't want to eat *here*!"

"Why? Isn't the food any good?"

She'd never tried it, actually. Between the no-free-food rule and the fact that everything they made was fifty percent grease, she'd never ventured past the diet soda. That wasn't important, though. The important thing was getting him away from there

97

as quickly as possible. If Mr. Roarke sent her to wipe Guy's table and ask him if his meal was "wienera-geous" she'd absolutely die.

"No," she said, straight-faced. "No, it isn't."

Melanie was leaving cheerleading practice when she caught sight of Jesse's red BMW in the parking lot outside the school gym. The athletes were al-lowed to park their cars there for after-school prac-tices, but that couldn't be Jesse's excuse—football had been over for weeks.

What's he doing here? she wondered. She wandered toward the edge of the parking lot, as drawn to the car as if it were Jesse himself. Dusk was already fall-ing, but there was still enough sunlight seeping into the black interior for Melanie to see that the vehicle was empty. She hesitated, then veered toward it across the asphalt, ignoring the fact that her bus stop was in the opposite direction.

There's no way he's in the library this late. And even if he were, why would he park over here? Could he be wait-ing for a friend on the basketball team? Who?

Jesse wasn't friendly with anyone on the team that she knew of. When he wasn't with Eight Prime he always hung out with his football friends. *Maybe he's just watching them practice.*

Why?

She didn't have a clue. Besides, she would have

noticed him if he'd been in the stands. The cheerleaders hadn't spent a lot of time in the main gym with the basketball team—it was too distracting to practice next to all those ball drills—but they'd been in there long enough. Jesse definitely hadn't been around then.

Melanie slowed her steps as she drew nearer to the BMW. The last rays of sunlight glinted off its back window while shadows from the trees on the rise in front of it reached out to claim the hood.

There was a movement in the trees.

Jesse. She could just make out his green jacket behind the edge of the largest trunk. But what was he doing?

She stopped, shading her eyes against the glare. Was he *hiding* behind that tree?

As she watched, Jesse's head inched back out. His eyes went first to a point up ahead of her, then scanned back to where she was standing and froze. He obviously hadn't expected her to be stopped in the middle of the lot, watching him. Even from that distance she could see his eyes widen. They stood that way a moment, their gazes locked; then slowly Jesse emerged from behind the tree.

His eyes never left hers as he walked down the shaded rise to the parking lot. His head broke into the sunshine as his feet reached the pavement, giving Melanie an even clearer view of his face. He looked at her defiantly, but there was something about his expression . . . something torn . . .

He misses me! she realized triumphantly. *That's what he's doing in the parking lot so late.*

Maybe he had only intended to spy on her as she left cheerleading practice, but she had caught him in the act—and it was time for his sulking to end. She already knew she wanted him back, and anyone who would go to such ridiculous lengths just to catch a glimpse of her obviously felt the same way.

She started toward him across the parking lot, the longing in her heart mirrored in his face. She had taken only a few steps, however, when a car drove between them and stopped.

"The bus stop's in the other direction," Vanessa Winters leaned over Tiffany Barrett to sneer out the passenger window. "Shouldn't you be waiting there with the other children?"

Tiffany giggled. "That's right! You're not *old* enough to drive, are you?"

"Get a life, Vanessa," Melanie retorted, sick to death of her cheerleading captain. Vanessa had been on her since the beginning of the year, in one way or another, but ever since their rivalry for Jesse had come into the open there was no more pretense of subtlety. "Why don't you go home and practice walking? Maybe then you'd get one of our patterns right."

Tiffany howled with laughter, and Vanessa looked

ready to explode. She opened her mouth to let Melanie have it, then abruptly shut it again, settling for punching the gas pedal until the engine roared. "Have fun taking the *bus*," she taunted, driving off in a cloud of exhaust.

Melanie glared as Vanessa's car disappeared. When she'd tried out for the squad, she'd thought cheerleading was going to solve all her problems. Instead, it had brought her a bunch of new ones. If not for their new coach, Sandra, she'd probably—

A door slammed, snapping Melanie back to the present. Jesse was starting his car! Before she could decide what to do, he backed out, spun around, and drove in the direction Vanessa had just gone, leaving Melanie behind.

"I ought to kill her!" Melanie exclaimed. Had it just been awful timing, or had Vanessa gotten between her and Jesse on purpose?

And what was Jesse's story? Why hadn't he waited?

Melanie shook her head angrily and began walking toward the bus stop.

He lost his nerve, she decided. The situation was delicate enough without Vanessa jumping into the middle of it. For a moment, she had been so close . . .

I'll see him tomorrow, she promised herself. *And when we get back together, this time I'll totally rub Vanessa's nose in it.*

Eight

She's got to be kidding me! Nicole thought, furious. Courtney Bell had just walked into the cafeteria with Emily I'm-So-Great Dooley, the two of them chatting and laughing like long-lost bosom buddies.

Not long-lost enough.

Nicole had been waiting near the end of the food line again that Tuesday, hoping to catch her best friend, but now she shrank into the crowd, desperate to avoid her while she figured out what to do.

Emily Dooley had moved into Clearwater Crossing during Nicole and Courtney's first year of junior high school, and at first Nicole had barely noticed her. She was quiet, for one thing, more part of the scenery than of the play, and her mouth was so full of braces she rarely smiled. To make things worse, her wardrobe in those days had been unremittingly pastel—safe pinks and dull blues, guaranteed not to stand out.

It had been a complete shock when Courtney had taken a shine to the girl. Courtney had been Courtney even back then, and not in the habit of cutting losers any slack. But whereas Nicole had written Emily off in the first five minutes, Courtney had seen something she hadn't.

Probably hero worship, Nicole thought bitterly, backing up until a wall stopped her progress. Safe in the shadow of the condiment station, she glared at Emily through narrowed eyes.

Sure, Emily looked all right now, but in junior high Courtney had been a fashion priestess compared to her. Courtney had made a game of making Emily over. She'd started with the hair—baby-fine, center part, a barrette on either side—convincing Emily to cut it short and spiky, then adding platinum blond streaks with a drugstore frost-and-tip kit. In Emily's brown hair, the crude streaks had stood out like frogs in a punch bowl. Nicole had been certain Mrs. Dooley would freak, but Emily had returned to school the next day, all tinny smiles, saying her mom was glad she was making friends.

Things had only gotten worse from there. It hadn't been long before Courtney was picking out Emily's clothes and teaching her all Nicole's makeup tricks. For Emily's part, she began to copy the way Courtney talked, the way Courtney walked—she even started drinking the same brand of soda. Nicole had found the entire situation nauseating. Didn't the girl have a mind of her own? More importantly, didn't she have any other friends?

Apparently not, because soon she was stuck to

Courtney like glue. At first Nicole had put up with her, annoyed that Courtney found it necessary to invite her everywhere but content in the knowledge that Emily wasn't a serious threat to their friendship. A clone like Emily could never be more than a third wheel. Or so Nicole had thought, until Courtney and Emily had begun making plans without her.

All-out war had followed.

Jealous, Nicole had quit speaking to Emily, had quit even *looking* at her, and she'd done everything she could think of to make Courtney follow her lead. Hours of scheming had been devoted to leaving Emily out of everything from a trip to the movies to a two-minute discussion by the drinking fountain.

Unfortunately, Emily hadn't taken Nicole's tactics lying down. Soon she was doing the same, only better, inviting Courtney on outings Nicole couldn't compete with: camping, water-skiing, a trip to the mall in St. Louis.

Nicole had retaliated by spreading juicy rumors about Emily.

Emily told a guy Nicole liked that Nicole practiced kissing on her pillow and pretended it was him.

Nicole put SpaghettiOs through the ventilation slots on Emily's locker . . .

Okay, it sounds immature now, but it was Emily's fault. She shouldn't have tried to take Courtney away.

In the end, when it had become painfully clear

that the three of them couldn't get along, Courtney had chosen Nicole.

Relieved to have her best friend back, Nicole hadn't gloated—much. She'd simply made it known that if Courtney had anything more to do with Emily the two of them would no longer be friends. She had been so jealous by that point that her rules had prohibited even simple hellos in the hall.

Ignored and abandoned, Emily had eventually moved on, gradually making new friends. By now the whole disaster was so buried in the past that Nicole had almost forgotten it.

Until today.

Her neck and shoulders tightened as she watched Emily and Courtney in the cafeteria line, schmoozing like seventh grade had never happened. Had Courtney gone crazy, to flaunt Emily in her face that way? Did she think Nicole didn't care anymore? Or was this her way of declaring war, of taking Nicole up on the threat she had made so many years before?

Didn't Court want to be her friend anymore?

This whole thing's ridiculous! thought Nicole, drawing a ragged breath. *Courtney's only doing this to make me jealous.*

And it was working really well.

"Are you working or daydreaming?" Peter asked.

They had barely arrived at his house after school

that Tuesday, barely begun their homework, and Jenna was already lost in space. "Huh?" she said, trying to focus on his amused smile.

"I guess that answers my question. I thought you were buried with homework."

Jenna sighed and leaned back in one of the Altmanns' padded den chairs. "I am. I have a ton. I just can't concentrate."

Peter put his notebook aside on the sofa. "Anything wrong?"

"No. Yes. But it's nothing new. Just Caitlin. Still."

"I thought you said she was coming around."

"A little, but she's still not happy with me. And even if she were, that doesn't fix things between her and David."

"I don't think there's anything to fix."

Jenna winced. "That's my point."

Peter shrugged. "I think you're just going to have to let nature take its course on this one. Admit it, Jenna, there are some things even you can't control."

"I know."

Peter sat up straighter. "Listen, not to change the subject, but I've been daydreaming about something too."

"Really? What?"

"An idea I had for the Junior Explorers. What do you think about summer day camp?"

"Summer anything sounds good to me," Jenna said with a sigh, turning her head toward the window. Outside, a cold rain was falling. "But we already do camp."

"Not a *day* camp," Peter said. "Not in Clearwater Crossing."

Jenna looked at him uncomprehendingly. Peter and his partner, college student Chris Hobart, had run a two-week camp at a church property on the Mississippi River for the last two summers. Not only had Jenna helped him do it, she knew summer camp was the main reason Peter had wanted the group to have a new bus, so he was sure of transportation for the long drive north.

"You want to do camp in *town* now, after we finally got the bus?"

"No, Jenna, you're not paying attention. We'll still do overnight camp at the river, but that only lasts two weeks. What I'm talking about is having camp all summer, but only during the day. We can use the bus to pick up the kids in the park in the morning, then take them back in the afternoon."

"Back from where?"

"That's the part I haven't figured out. It ought to be someplace fun, though. We can't spend the entire summer at the park."

"I don't see why not. With all that sports equipment we bought we could finally use the ball fields and basketball courts. And in the summer they stock that pond in the corner. The kids could go fishing."

"True," Peter said thoughtfully. "But no one's

allowed to swim there. Maybe we could spend some days at the park, and other days somewhere else."

"Like where?" Jenna repeated.

Peter shrugged. "Beats me. The lake?"

"Wouldn't we have to have lifeguards? At the river they have lifeguards."

"Well, I didn't say I had this all worked out. I just said I was dreaming about it."

"Oh."

Jenna dreamed about it a minute too, until Peter excused himself and headed down the hall to the bathroom. Then her thoughts went back to Caitlin. If she only knew how David felt, she'd be in a much better position to tell her sister what to do.

Oh wow, she thought, her heart beating faster. *That's it!*

Peter was going to be busy for a few minutes. David's room was just down the hall . . .

Rising quickly, Jenna crept to the den doorway and peeked cautiously into the hall. Mrs. Altmann was still reading in the living room—Jenna could see the glow of a lamp and hear a newspaper rustle. In the opposite direction, way down at the end, the bathroom door was shut. Holding her breath, Jenna tiptoed down the hall, straight to David's room. She hesitated in the open doorway a second, afraid Peter would come out of the bathroom and catch her spying, then made up her mind and stepped inside.

She had never been in David's room before, only

glimpsed the interior during random trips up and down the hall, but she remembered that when David had lived at home the room had been constantly changing. One time the windowsill would be full of antique bottles; another, tennis trophies. The bed moved from the hall wall to an end wall. The sports and music posters were rotated month by month to keep up with changing interests. And always there were books, sneakers, jackets, and laundry scattered every which way, giving the place a sense of life. Since David had gone off to college, however, the room seemed to have frozen in time. He still slept there when he came home, but he had apparently lost interest in changing things around, as if it were no longer truly his room.

Jenna crept forward, her gaze scanning the bed, the dresser, the windowsill. She didn't even know what she was looking for. Just anything. Any little clue about Mary Beth or Caitlin . . .

The closet was closed and she didn't dare open it, but there was a collage of photos over the desk. Rushing to it eagerly, Jenna scanned the faces, looking for one of her sisters. The photos were all old and faded, though. No help whatsoever. And Peter was going to be coming down the hall any second. . . .

Unsure what more she could do, Jenna stood in the middle of David's room and made one slow turn. Nothing. The room was so picked up, so put away, it seemed more like a museum exhibit than a place to live. There wasn't a speck of dust anywhere, and the bed was so tightly made the spread could have bounced a quarter. Jenna almost expected to see an explanatory plaque on the wall or hear a tour group bearing down on her.

Heaving a frustrated sigh, she poked her head into the hall and made sure the bathroom door was still shut before she ventured out. On her way back to the den, though, she paused to glance into Peter's room.

The furniture and layout were basically the same, but in contrast to the sterility of David's, Peter's room looked chaotic, comfortable, lived in. Books and papers were scattered everywhere, and his bed was more smoothed over than made. Hanging above the pillows, like a luminous small window, was the framed watercolor Melanie had painted for him after her accident.

Jenna always felt the sight of that picture like a splash of cold water in the face. Peter insisted that Melanie had given it to him only out of friendship, that it didn't mean anything, but Jenna was pretty sure that none of Melanie's other "friends" in Eight Prime had ever received a painting. She was *positive* none of them had been Melanie's date for the homecoming formal. Maybe Peter had never thought of Melanie romantically, but Jenna would never know what Melanie had thought—even considering the possibilities filled her with dread. If Jenna hadn't realized what she was losing and fixed things with Peter when she did, maybe he'd be Melanie's boyfriend now. Just like David was going to be Mary Beth's if Caitlin didn't act fast....

She needs to speak up, Jenna thought, still staring at the evidence of her own near disaster. It was so obvious to her.

Why couldn't Caitlin see it?

When Jesse pulled up to the parking lot exit after school, Melanie was waiting for him. The moment he stopped at the stop sign, she stepped out in front of his car, blocking his way. The rain that had started falling after lunchtime pelted down on her hood, but she held her ground, staring at him through his streaming windshield.

Jesse looked at her disbelievingly. His side window went down with a mechanical hum.

"What are you doing?" he yelled over the weather. "I'm trying to drive." The longing Melanie thought she had seen in his eyes the day before had been replaced by pure irritation.

"I need a ride," she called back anyway.

"What's wrong with the bus?"

"I don't want to take the bus. I want to talk to you."

He seemed about to refuse, but there were cars behind his now. The nearest one started honking.

"I'm not moving," Melanie warned him.

Jesse rose in his seat, then sank back down, defeated, as more horns sounded impatiently. "Get in, then," he said through his teeth. "And for Pete's sake, hurry up."

Climbing into the black leather seat, Melanie tried not to think about what she was doing to his upholstery. Rain ran in rivulets down her coat, spilling onto the floor mats. She pushed her wet hood off her head as Jesse pulled out into traffic, his gaze fixed steadfastly ahead.

"Jesse, we have to talk," she began, less confidently than she'd intended.

"No. We don't."

"You don't even know what I want to talk about."

"What if I don't care?"

He *had* to care. He always had before. "What if you do?"

Jesse snorted as he guided his car along the rain-washed street. The weather outside made the warm, protected interior of the BMW seem like its own little world. "All right. Let's hear it."

I'm so sorry. I was wrong.

Melanie had to strain not to shout out the words she'd been thinking for so long. With Jesse still so angry, though, she didn't have the courage to be so direct.

"I, uh, I thought about you while I was in L.A.," she said. "I thought about you the whole time."

"Pretty boring trip, huh?" Jesse said sarcastically.

"Not at all. Why do you always think the worst?"

"Gee, I don't know. Past experience?"

"For your information, I had a great time. I could have, anyway. I met this guy named Brad and he took me to the beach and the observatory and all over Holly—"

"I can see you were really missing me." Jesse's blue eyes snapped angrily as he finally looked her way. "I don't know what you're thinking, Melanie, but if you think I care in the slightest what you do or who you see, you're seriously mistaken. Run around with all the losers you like—I'm not exactly sitting home pining."

"No," Melanie groaned. As usual, he didn't get it. The only reason she had even mentioned Brad was to prove she wasn't thinking about Jesse simply for something to do. Leave it to Jesse to fly off the handle before he even knew what she was driving at.

"Jesse, that wasn't the point."

They were nearing the turnoff onto the Andrewses' private road. If she didn't want to blow this chance, she had to talk fast. "It was dating Brad that made me realize how much I missed *you.*"

His expression showed how little he believed her. "Well, no one can expect to snag anyone too hot in just seventy-two hours. Not even you."

"Will you pay attention? He was *totally* hot. Half the girls at school would *walk* to California for the chance to go out with this guy."

Jesse hit the brakes too hard in her wet driveway. The car slid forward, barely missing the garage. "I hope the two of you will be very happy."

"Jesse—"

"I've got things to do today, Melanie. So if you'll just get out of my car . . ."

Her hand closed on the door handle. The way Jesse was treating her, she knew she ought to be *thrilled* to get out of his car.

"Do you want to come in?" she blurted out instead.

He looked at her if she were crazy. "I just said I had to go."

"I know. But I thought . . . well . . . never mind."

In the rain outside, she slammed his passenger door, not bothering to run for the shelter of her doorway or even to put up her hood as she watched him drive away. She couldn't help remembering the beginning of the school year, when he had constantly angled for invitations while she had barely tolerated him.

A trickle of ice water ran down her neck, making Melanie shiver. *Things sure have changed since September.*

Nine

"Are you comfortable?" Miguel asked.

"Sure. Aren't you?" said Leah.

Neither one of them was comfortable. That much was obvious by the inanity of their conversation.

"I just thought you might be cold." He twitched more of the stadium blanket they were sharing over her legs. "It's colder up here than I thought it would be. Maybe we ought to go back."

For the second time that week, Leah was at the lake. But whereas on Monday she'd driven up there to brood by herself, that Wednesday she was there with Miguel, who had taken a rare day off from work. She'd been so excited by the prospect of some time alone with him that she hadn't even told him she'd been there two days before, remembering instead the first time she and Miguel had gone to the lake to-gether, and the way she had kissed his tears dry. . . .

"I don't want to go back," she said, snuggling closer despite the gearshift between them.

Granted, she had hoped to walk around—or at least get out of the car—but although the rain had stopped, a cold wind was blowing over the lake, whipping its surface into steely ripples. *Never mind*, she thought. *There are things we can do right here.*

She stretched out a tentative hand, but it had barely left her lap when he twisted around in his seat.

"I've, uh, I've been wanting to ask you something," he said.

His handsome face was framed like a picture in the gray sky of the window behind him, but his anxious tone made her cringe. "What?"

"Would you want to raise your children Jewish, Christian, or neither, like you?"

"Who says I'm neither?" Leah drew back her hand, offended. "Maybe I'm both."

Miguel made a face. "You can't be *both*."

"Are you sure?"

"I'm . . . well . . ." He shook his head, obviously not ready to debate her. "It was a simple question, Leah."

"No, it wasn't. Besides, what do you mean *my* children? If you're talking about *our* children, why don't you come out and say so?"

"I just, uh—"

"Why are we even talking about children?" she asked irritably. "We're practically still children ourselves."

"I just . . . never mind. Forget I asked."

As if *that* were remotely possible. Leah crossed her arms over her chest, more convinced than ever that

Miguel was looking for a way out. Instead of beating around the bush, why didn't he just admit it?

"You know what?" she said, her voice as cool as the weather. "I *do* think we ought to go back.

"Another excellent shift, Gail!" Mr. Roarke beamed at his favorite. "I don't know what I'd do without you."

"Oh, Mr. Roarke." Gail giggled delightedly. "You probably say that to everyone."

He doesn't say it to me, Nicole thought sullenly, not sure whether to feel slighted or be glad. Sometimes the way their boss looked at Gail was actually kind of gross.

Reaching behind her for the doorknob, Nicole let herself into the break room to change out of her uniform. The Wednesday shift was over, and she'd be crazy if she wasted another minute in that dump while Gail and Mr. Roarke held their mutual admiration session in the hall. Nicole had barely shut the door, however, when it flew open again, Gail framed in the doorway.

"Oh, Mr. Roarke, you're so funny," Gail cooed, backing into the room. "But I have to get ready or I'll miss my ride."

She locked the door and then, to Nicole's surprise, pressed her ear to the wood and froze in position.

"What are you doing?" Nicole asked.

Gail made a face and waved for her to be quiet.

"What do you think?" Nicole persisted. "That he's standing out there spying on us?"

Gail's eyes opened wide and her waving became downright frantic. Astonished by her cousin's behavior, Nicole fell silent, afraid even to unzip her backpack for fear of triggering another fit.

At last Gail stepped away from the door. "He's gone," she said, her voice slightly hushed. "I think he went back to the kitchen."

"Did you think he was out there listening?"

"Are you kidding?" Gail took off her hat and shook out her black hair. "I *know* he was listening. Mr. Dork eavesdrops on everyone."

She slipped her tunic off over her head, then fished a sweater and pair of pants out of her backpack and began putting them on.

"Mr. *Who*?" Nicole asked, trying not to crack up. The enormity of the other information was completely lost with Gail's slip of the tongue.

But Gail only smiled in return. "You *are* new, aren't you? Everyone calls him that. Most people think of it themselves by the second or third day."

Nicole hung her head. Now that she'd heard Gail say it, it did seem kind of obvious.

"Why, Mr. *Dork*!" Gail trilled unexpectedly, waltzing across the break room in her stocking feet. Her pink lips puckered as she batted her thick lashes over modestly lowered eyes. "You are absolutely the funniest, most handsomest, most manliest thing alive!" she drawled in what Nicole could only assume was a bad try at Scarlett O'Hara.

Bad . . . ridiculous . . . and more than a little amusing. Nicole smiled uncertainly as she tried to take it all in. Gail was turning out to be a lot more complex than she had remembered.

On the other hand, where did her cousin get off making fun of the boss after all her kissing up? Maybe this was some type of sick test the two of them had invented. Maybe Mr. Dork—uh, Roarke—*was* standing outside the door, just waiting to see if Nicole would go along.

"I don't think you ought to be doing that," Nicole said dubiously.

Gail looked put out. "Why? Are you going to tell on me?"

"Noooo . . ." Nicole's eyes drifted toward the door.

"What?" Gail glanced that way too, a puzzled expression on her face. Suddenly her confusion cleared.

"Oh, I get it. He's not out there." She snapped back the bolt and opened the door so Nicole could see for herself. The hallway was empty, as Gail had promised. She locked the door again. "What do you think? I'm crazy?"

Nicole didn't want to tell her what she had thought. "I thought you *liked* Mr. Roarke," she said instead.

Gail stared. "That little pervert? What made you think that?"

Pervert? It was Nicole's turn to stare as Gail sat down to pull on her boots. "Well . . . uh, you're always smiling at him and laughing at his jokes. And you do whatever he tells you."

"I've got a news flash for you, Nicole: That little dweeb's the boss. Not only that, but *his* boss is my dad's best friend. That's why I kiss his butt, and since my dad is your dad's brother, you might want to try it yourself. I've always found that if you want adults off your case, brownnosing's a good skill to master."

Nicole let her backpack drop to the floor, completely forgetting she'd come there to change. Gail *knew* she was kissing up? Nicole had always thought her cousin's groveling an unconscious reflex, as natural to her as breathing. The mere possibility that she did it on purpose was positively disorienting.

"I—I don't think I could do that," Nicole stammered.

"Oh, sure you could. It's easy."

Gail stood up and pretended to address an imaginary third person. "That is *such* a good idea!" she exclaimed, nodding at the empty air. "Wow! I'm going to get on that right away."

She turned back to Nicole. "Okay, now you try."

Nicole felt stupid, but Gail was looking at her so expectantly she didn't know what else to do.

"Uh, I'll do that right away," she repeated.

120

"That one was too easy," Gail said, a mischievous twinkle entering her eyes. "Try this."

Her expression changed in an instant, to one of total contrition. "I know. You're right. If I only listened to you more often my life would be a lot easier."

"Huh?"

"For your dad, of course. Or your mom. You really have to watch your delivery on that one, but if you nail it it works every time."

"Are you kidding me?" Nicole demanded.

Gail smiled. "All right. Just most of the time. It's killer for getting the car keys."

"Gail! I've *heard* you say those types of things, and I can't believe you weren't serious."

Her cousin laughed with obvious glee. "If people didn't think I was serious, I'd be wasting my time, wouldn't I?"

"Um . . . well . . ."

"Oh, loosen up, Nicole. Do you *always* have to be so good?"

"Me! It's *you*! *You're* the good one."

"Really?" Gail seemed delighted. "You think I'm the good one?"

"Duh, Gail. *Everyone* thinks you're the good one."

"Cool! I'm even better than I thought, then." Gail pulled her coat on over her street clothes, and Nicole suddenly realized that while she'd been gaping like a fish out of water her cousin had finished changing.

"Well, it looks like I'm out of here." Gail smiled as she reached for the doorknob. "I know how much you love that uniform, Nicole, but unless you're wearing it home you'd better hurry up and change. Mr. Roarke will be here in a minute, wanting to know what's taking so long."

"What does he care? I'm off the clock."

Gail screwed up her face until it looked like a lemon had lodged in her windpipe. "Here at Wiener-ageous, there's no such thing as off the clock," she declared in a dead-on imitation of Mr. Roarke. "Our conduct in this building reflects the Wienerageous ideal at *all* times."

"He never said that."

Gail giggled. "Not yet. I haven't suggested it yet." She threw the door open with a flourish. "Catch you later!"

Nicole stood staring at her cousin's retreating back. Was that girl really Gail, Miss Excruciatingly Perfect?

Change the coal black hair to red, and she could almost be Courtney's twin.

At least she could be if she had Emily Dooley growing out of her hip.

Nicole's teeth clenched at the memory of her best friend and her worst enemy eating lunch together again that day.

If I ever speak to Courtney again, that girl has a lot of explaining to do.

Ten

"Can't you blow this off?" Sabrina asked. "I mean, I don't mind letting you off early, but don't you have enough to do already without taking on a charity?"

Miguel's back was to Sabrina, but he didn't slow his pace as he cleaned his painting tools. "I'm not 'taking on' a charity. I've been involved with Eight Prime since September."

"Can't you drop it?"

Miguel snapped the lid onto the can of paint he'd been using and turned to face her. "I don't want to drop it. We started this group to remember Kurt Englbehrt, and it's important to me."

"Oh, right. The bus thing." Sabrina nodded slowly as understanding dawned. "But didn't you already buy that? I saw on TV how the city council put up the money."

"They put up *half* the money," Miguel corrected testily. He didn't have time to go into details about how hard Eight Prime had worked to buy that bus for the Junior Explorers, but he wasn't about to let those

123

jerks on the council steal their glory, either. "Not *even* half, by the time you count taxes and painting Kurt's name on the bus."

"So if you already have the bus, how come you guys are still meeting?"

"We're in the hole," Miguel said impatiently. He appreciated Sabrina's letting him off a half hour early, but if she was going to talk the whole time it wasn't much help. "We need to keep a fund for gas and bus maintenance—things like that."

"Oh. Still, I can't believe you go to school, have a job, and do a charity too."

If she only knew, Miguel thought, imagining how much more complicated his life would get if he and Leah became engaged. They had made up their fight of the day before, but everything else was still up in the air.

"What about water polo?" Sabrina persisted. "Aren't you on the team this year?"

"That doesn't start until spring." He edged a little closer to the door. "Look, I really have to get moving. I'll see you tomorrow. No, wait—Saturday, right?"

"Saturday," Sabrina agreed as he flew out the door, reaching the office building's main exit in only a few long strides.

But her last question dogged him as he ran through the dark to his car. There was no way he could play water polo if he was as busy when the season started as he'd been for the last few weeks. And spring wasn't that far away. . . .

I can still do it, he reassured himself, fumbling with his car keys. *Jesse was on the football team and in Eight Prime at the same time.*

He dropped into the driver's seat and coaxed the cold engine to life.

Of course, Jesse didn't have to work—and he definitely wasn't engaged.

Maybe he could cut back on his work hours a little, just for the length of the season. His mother wouldn't mind. But if he needed to start saving for a wedding . . .

It will all work out, Miguel thought, steering his old car into the street.

At least I hope it will.

"What's in that big envelope?" Jenna asked the moment Melanie climbed into Peter's Toyota.

"It's a surprise." Melanie settled into the backseat and smiled to herself as Jenna's mouth pursed with suspense.

"What kind of surprise?"

"If I tell you, then where's the surprise?"

"Dangling a surprise in front of Jenna is like showing a red flag to a bull," Peter teased as he drove. "In case you haven't noticed, she has a little problem with curiosity."

Melanie caught the way he smiled at his girlfriend

when he said it, though, and had to fight back a pang. She tried hard to be happy for Peter and Jenna, but there was no denying she still sometimes wished things had gone a different way.

"Actually, it's a present. For you, Nicole, and Leah."

"A present!" Jenna wailed. "Now you *have* to tell me."

"Don't you think we ought to wait until we get to Jesse's?" Melanie countered.

"No. It'll be more fun if you let me see it now and let the others see it later. Right? That spreads out the fun."

"I don't know. . . ."

"Pleeeease?" Jenna begged, hanging over the back of her seat.

"Yes," Peter echoed. "Please. Otherwise this is going to be the longest ten-minute ride of our lives."

"You won't even be able to see in the car. It's too dark."

Jenna flipped on the overhead light, her expression so hopeful that Melanie finally relented.

"All right," she said, pulling one of three eight-by-ten color photographs out of the envelope and handing it to Jenna. "Here's yours."

"Oh, look!" Jenna squealed. "How cute!"

"What is it?" Peter took his eyes off the road long enough to peek at the picture Jenna turned his way.

"It's Tom Cruise's star," Jenna explained. "From

the Hollywood Walk of Fame. Remember how I told you Nicole thought she saw Tom Cruise and we chased that poor guy and his girlfriend?"

Melanie stared out the window, watching the dark streets slip by as Jenna told Peter what had happened after that, when the girls had stumbled onto Tom's star during their tour of Hollywood Boulevard. She had never been to Jesse's house before, and there was no denying the nervous lump growing in her stomach.

What if he says something rude to me in front of the rest of Eight Prime? she worried. *Or worse, refuses to speak to me at all?*

Not that either of those things would probably be that noteworthy. She and Jesse had sparred or ignored each other through so many different Eight Prime meetings that it was almost a tradition.

At last Peter parked in front of a giant Tudor mansion. The knot in Melanie's gut turned to butterflies as she walked up the long stone path to the door.

So this is where Jesse lives.

People were always a little amazed by her house, but Jesse's was just as impressive—in a totally different way. Broad and facing the street from an even broader lawn, the light gray facade stretched up to a second story, then ended in a roof with a series of peaks. Melanie reached the wide stone stoop and hesitated in front of the oak double doors. Leaded, beveled glass panels in the top halves let the light shine out from within, and she was trying to find a clear angle for a look inside when an extra-loud chime made her jump.

"Wow," Peter said, chuckling as he took his finger off the doorbell. "That ought to get somebody out here."

"Yeah, like a butler," Jenna whispered, awed. "I had no idea his house was so big. I think it's even bigger than yours, Melanie."

Melanie shrugged. "From the front," she acknowledged, refraining from mentioning that hers sat on several acres.

She had no sooner spoken than a shape appeared behind the leaded glass. A girl in a plaid Catholic-school jumper and Mickey Mouse slippers opened the door and peered out at the trio from a large, wood-paneled entry.

"You must be Brittany," Melanie said quickly, thinking it might help her case with Jesse to win his stepsister over. "I'm Melanie, and this is Peter and Jenna."

"Hello," they said.

Brittany sized them up before her eyes came back to Melanie. "Jesse!" she yelled. "Your friends are here."

"Is anyone else here yet?" Peter asked.

Brittany shook her head. "You're the first ones. *Jesse!*"

Jesse didn't appear, but a tall, thin woman with

frosted blond hair came into the entry from a side door. "Don't just stand there screaming, darling. Invite them in."

She turned a superficial smile on the guests. "Hello, I'm Jesse's mother, Elsa. I'm sure Jesse will be down in a second, so why don't I just show you all to the den?"

Melanie made sure to be at the front of the line as they followed Elsa through the house. Passing details caught her attention—an oak-railed staircase, a mahogany dining table, an enormous Boston fern on a wooden stand—but her primary interest was in Jesse's flashy stepmom.

"I'm Melanie," she volunteered as Elsa led them along.

Elsa smiled vacantly, making Melanie pretty sure she'd never heard of her before.

"You're a cheerleader," Brittany said unexpectedly.

"That's right!" Melanie replied, flashing her a big smile. Maybe it was a waste of effort impressing people Jesse didn't even like, but she didn't see how it could hurt.

The den looked like something from a Victorian hotel, all dark wood and red upholstery with a wall of tiny-paned windows. A silver-haired man sat reading in a leather recliner, a pile of books and magazines spilling from his lap.

"Clint, honey, you're going to have to move now," Elsa told him. "Jesse's little friends are here."

"What?" Dr. Jones said irritably. "Where the hell is Jesse?"

Melanie exchanged uncomfortable glances with Peter and Jenna.

"I don't know, dear. He's *your* son."

"I told him I had to catch up on my research in here. Why can't he do this in the living room?"

Elsa moved closer to the chair and turned her back on the teens. "I already told you," she said in a voice that was low but not low enough. "I won't have a bunch of kids in my living room, eating on my good furniture. You're the one who told him he could have his little party here, so you'll just have to move to your study."

Dr. Jones looked as though he had a wealth of things to say on that subject. He opened his mouth, then looked past Elsa and locked eyes with Melanie. She could see him reconsider as he realized every word was being overheard.

"Oh, all right," he said grudgingly. Cranking the recliner up to a sitting position, he began gathering his things. "But I'm not going to get anything done in the study with a bunch of kids hanging out right next door. I'll have to work somewhere else."

"Do you really have to work tonight?"

Dr. Jones looked askance at his much younger wife. "Of course. What else would I do?"

A squeaking of sneakers on the wood parquet be-

130

hind them made Melanie turn her head. Jesse had just appeared in the doorway, his short hair still wet from the shower. "You guys are early," he said.

"Are we?" Peter checked his watch. "I guess. A couple of minutes."

"I was just . . ." Jesse trailed off and turned to his father. "So am I using this room or what?"

"Yes, hold your horses. We were all just leaving."

Melanie couldn't help noticing the way Elsa stalked out of the den ahead of her husband. Her daughter stayed close to her heels, her head tilted back at the same haughty angle.

"You, uh . . . you kids have fun," Dr. Jones mumbled to Jesse before he went out.

Jesse shut the door quickly behind them, taking a long, deep breath before he faced his friends. "Sorry about that," he said, looking at Peter and Jenna.

"No problem," Jenna said quickly. "We shouldn't have come early."

But as Melanie helped herself to a chair, she wondered how Jesse had known he needed to apologize for his family when he hadn't even been there. Had he seen some telltale sign—or was an apology that automatic?

We're the same, she thought, feeling more destined to be with him than ever. *Just a couple of rich kids rattling around in big houses, trying to hide broken hearts.*

And if there were a couple more people in Jesse's

mansion than hers, it didn't change how alone he obviously was. *No wonder he drinks—it's a miracle I don't.*

She studied him closely as he hustled around, pulling sodas from a paneled refrigerator and filling a bowl with chips. He was still pretending not to notice her, but she could feel the tension between them, pulling like a tide.

Maybe he really is the one.

Maybe between them there were still enough pieces of a heart left to patch together something they both could use.

"You mean we'd be like *counselors?*" Nicole demanded. "Every day? All summer?"

Peter had just broken his idea of a summer day camp to the assembled members of Eight Prime.

Jenna wasn't surprised by Nicole's reaction— she'd have been surprised if it had been different— but as the unofficial secretary of the group she scribbled it down with her trusty pink pen and prepared to record the comments of the others.

"How are we going to pay for so much gas?" Miguel asked.

"You can't just drive them around with nowhere to go," Jesse said. "If you want to have a camp, you need some sort of base."

"That would be best," said Melanie. "That way you'd have tables, and chairs, and storage. Not to mention somewhere for the kids to change into their bathing suits."

"I wonder if someone might let us use a vacant property somewhere?" Leah mused. "Just for the summer."

"I was thinking on the lake would be—" Peter began.

"We could have uniforms!" Ben cried excitedly. "Like ranger hats, and shorts with lots of pockets and—"

"What about bathrooms?" Leah said. "I'll take a bathroom over a goofy hat any day."

"You *have* to have bathrooms," Nicole agreed. "With all those kids? Come on."

"Wait! Wait, you guys. I can't keep up," Jenna broke in, scribbling frantically. "You're all talking way too fast."

"How much did you get?" Ben practically fell into her lap in his eagerness to read from beside her on the couch. "Did you get that part about the uniforms?"

"Yes. Wait." Her pen kept moving at top speed, even in the silence. "All right, I got it. But slow down!"

"If we took the easels from the park, we could set up an arts and crafts area," Melanie said. "It wouldn't cost much to get a load of new paints and paper."

"Don't fool yourself," Miguel said darkly. "This whole project is going to cost plenty."

133

"You know what would be cool?" Jesse said. "What if we could rent a property that had a boathouse and a dock? Then the kids could swim off the dock, and we could use the building to store all the sports equipment and stuff."

"I *still* think we're going to need a lifeguard," Jenna said, writing away.

Leah nodded. "Good point."

"We could buy a ski boat!" Ben shouted. "If we put our minds to it, I know we could do it."

"No doubt," Peter said with a smile. "But I was thinking more along the lines of half a dozen inner tubes."

"With hikes in the woods," Jenna interjected again.

"Baseball games," Jesse said.

"Are we really doing this?" Nicole demanded. "Or is this all just a big fantasy?"

"It's kind of a fantasy right now," Peter admitted. "Especially if you look at our bank account."

He stood up to pass out sheets showing their recent expenditures and current balance: $1.41. "I actually had to put in twenty dollars myself to keep us from going below zero."

"We'll pay you back," Melanie said quickly, laying her paper aside. "We're here to plan a fund-raiser anyway, right? I even have an idea."

"Let's hear it," said Leah, leaning forward.

134

"It's just a couple of weeks until Valentine's Day. I think we ought to sell candy and flowers at school."

"That won't work," Miguel said immediately. "No offense, but we'd have to have some money already to buy the stuff to sell."

Jenna could tell by her expression that Melanie hadn't thought of that. Even so, she came back quickly.

"What if we used our own money? I mean, everyone still has some cash hanging around from Christmas, right? We'll just keep track of what each person puts in, and after the sale we'll pay ourselves back."

"I've got fifty bucks!" Ben volunteered. "We probably only need a couple hundred."

Nicole shook her head. "Two hundred might be enough for suckers, but not for chocolates."

"Suckers are a great idea!" said Jenna. "They're little, so we'll be able to carry a lot of them, and we can split them up between us."

"How about carnations for the flowers?" Leah said. "They do better out of water than roses, and they come in good Valentine's colors."

"I like peppermint," Ben said. "You know, the one that's all red and white streaks? Let's get peppermint."

"Why not mix them up?" Melanie suggested. "We could get some of those, and plain red, pink, and white, too."

"White's boring," Nicole declared.

"White's classic," Melanie shot back.

A long debate about flowers ensued, followed by one about buckets, then whether it was better to buy a commercial floral preservative or use Mrs. Brewster's special recipe of aspirins and 7UP. There were a million details to settle: when, where, who, and how—the only thing they already knew was why. By the time they'd finally hashed out a plan, Jenna's wrist was aching.

"Okay, is that it then?" she asked hopefully. "I think we all know what to do, at least for now."

"We ought to have another meeting next week," Melanie said.

Peter rose from his chair. "Sounds good to me. Okay with everyone else?"

"Yes," they all said together.

"Maybe we should meet for lunch next week too," Leah said. "This is coming up pretty fast, and we ought to get progress reports."

"Let's meet in the cafeteria on Tuesday," Miguel suggested. "Bring sack lunches—it'll save time on waiting in line."

"This is going to be great!" Ben said, rubbing his hands together. "Eight Prime strikes again!"

Eleven

"Are you waiting for the bus?" Gail asked, following Nicole out to the sidewalk after their Friday shift.

The sky was dark, the weather freezing, but Nicole's grimace was from embarrassment. "Yes."

"If you want, we could give you a ride."

"We?"

"I'm waiting for someone to pick me up. He likes to drive, so I doubt he'll mind dropping you off."

Nicole raised an eyebrow. Clearwater Crossing and Mapleton were in opposite directions, so Nicole's house would be pretty far out of the way. Not to mention Gail's use of the pronoun *he*. Was she trying to say she had a date? Before Nicole could ask, a black Camaro appeared at the curb, honking despite the fact that it was no more than six feet away.

"There's Neil," Gail said, skipping toward the car. "Come on."

Nicole hiked her backpack higher on her shoulder but stayed where she was. The last few days had made her change some of her beliefs about Gail, but she was still almost afraid to imagine the kind of loser her cousin would attract.

He'll be the brainy type, Nicole predicted as Gail pulled the passenger door open and leaned down to talk to her friend.

On the other hand, he did have a pretty cool car.

"Come on!" Gail called again. "Neil says it's all right."

Nicole hesitated, then made up her mind. Anything was better than riding the bus.

But when she ducked her head to climb into the back, she almost died from the shock. Neil was a *babe*! A *college-age* babe. With tattoos on both forearms.

"So you're Gail's cousin," he said with a mocking smile. "Geez. You couldn't prove it by me."

Nicole buckled her seat belt in a daze.

"Be nice," Gail told him as she shut her door. "Don't pick on Nicole."

"I'm not picking on her, Jelly. I'm just saying. You two don't have much in common."

That's all right, then, Nicole thought, relieved. Even this total stranger could see how much cooler she was than Gail.

"Then again, who could compete with my Jelly?" *Huh?*

He reached across the gearshift to poke Gail in the ribs. She screamed, but instead of twisting away from his tickling threw herself into his arms. Nicole was shocked enough that her prissy cousin knew a guy like Neil. That he called her Jelly was even weirder. But the sight of the kiss Gail laid on his lips . . .

There was absolutely no space between their bodies. Neil's hands were everywhere, and Gail was practically climbing into his lap. Nicole suddenly realized she'd stopped breathing. She averted her eyes and sucked in air as the blood flooded into her cheeks. Where had Gail learned to kiss like *that*?

"Hey, I got us some food," Gail said, breaking out of the clinch.

"Killer."

Neil pulled away from the curb in the direction of Clearwater Crossing, while Gail bent to open her backpack.

"I couldn't get drinks," she said, straightening up with a stuffed paper bag. "But I have hot dogs and burgers and fries."

"Let me have a dog," Neil said, driving with his left hand and holding out his right.

Gail turned the wrapper partway down on a hot dog, making it into a neat package before she handed it to her boyfriend. "You want something to eat, Nicole?"

"No, that's okay. I—"

"Oh, come on. I've got tons of stuff here, and I'm not even that hungry."

Nicole thought only another second. "A burger, then."

She had to admit to an increasing curiosity about

what the food at Wienerageous tasted like, and since Gail had already bought this batch, there was no point in letting it go to waste. Nicole peeled back the paper on the hamburger and took a tentative bite.

The taste of spicy mustard exploded in her mouth, followed by high notes of pickles and onions. The lettuce crunched crisply; the tomato was firm and ripe. And underneath it all was the burger itself, juicy and charbroiled, dressed in a blanket of thick, gooey cheese.

"Oh, this is *good*," she said, licking mustard from her lip.

"Yeah, not bad," Gail agreed, tearing the paper on one of her own. "The uniforms suck, but at least we don't have to be ashamed of the food."

"Are the hot dogs as good as the hamburgers?"

"The chili dog is the best," Neil said. "Didn't you get any chili dogs, Jelly?"

Gail shook her head. "I couldn't this time."

"Aw, man. Pass me some french fries, then."

Gail passed out fries three ways. For a couple of minutes, the only sounds in the car were rustling and chewing. Nicole kept telling herself that she shouldn't eat the whole burger, that she shouldn't even *taste* the fries, but everything was so tempting, and in the end she gave in.

What difference does it make? she thought, stuffing greasy potatoes into her mouth. The Hollywood photograph Melanie had given her the night before loomed in her mind as she chewed. Jenna and Leah had seemed thrilled with their copies, and Nicole supposed it was a pretty good picture, but the hidden message it contained had mocked her the moment she saw it.

Remember Wake-up Day? it said. *This was the day you found out that you're no more a model than this concrete is Tom Cruise.*

Nicole cringed anew at the bitter memory.

Eat the hamburger, she thought, taking another bite. *Eat a hamburger a day. What difference does it make?*

"I wish you'd gotten the chili dogs," Neil said petulantly.

"Have a burger," Gail offered.

"It's not the same."

"Well, I'm sorry, but it's hard enough sneaking in and out of that kitchen without stopping to rattle around in the chili pot. If you want a chili dog so bad, you'll have to come in and pay for it."

Nicole stopped eating in midbite. Was Gail saying what she thought she was saying?

"I can't believe your boss is such a tightwad," Neil complained, taking the hamburger. "I've never heard of a restaurant where they don't let employees eat the food."

"Mr. Dork's fifth rule of continued employment," Gail said, twisting around in her seat to face Nicole.

141

"Okay, now, what is it?" she coaxed in the oversweet, overpatient voice she'd used that first day of training. She didn't wait for Nicole's answer. "No free food for anyone, ever!" she cried, in a perfect imitation of their boss.

But this time Nicole didn't find her cousin's act so funny. She put down her half-eaten burger, the other half lead in her belly.

"Do you mean you didn't pay for these?"

Gail tossed her head impatiently. "For the pathetic wages that miser pays us, we ought to be allowed to stuff ourselves whenever we want."

Nicole sat speechless, unable to believe her cousin would go so far—or that she was now guilty by association. She wished with all her heart that she had ridden the bus the way she was supposed to. For a moment she even thought the stolen food she'd just eaten was in danger of coming back up.

"You've got to hear this new CD," Gail said, turning back to Neil. "I just got it yesterday and I already love it."

Seconds later, a crash of heavy metal filled the Camaro's interior.

"Crank it up!" Gail commanded, spinning the volume dial to a point that made conversation impossible.

Bouncing along with the music, she leaned over to kiss Neil. The Camaro swerved into the oncoming lane.

"Hey, Jelly. You wench," Neil growled, pushing her away. "You're going to make me wreck."

Gail laughed and bounced back into her seat. "Fine. Who needs you?"

Pulling a cigarette out of her backpack, she lit up. "Cigarette, Nicole?" she shouted, offering the pack over the back of her seat.

"No. Uh, Gail, don't you think taking food from work is a little, well . . . risky?"

"Of course—if I was stupid enough to get caught."

"Or if your little cousin squeals on you," Neil said.

For the first time, Gail looked concerned. "You wouldn't, would you?" she asked, peering into Nicole's eyes. "That would be really uncool."

"I—I'm not going to tell."

"I didn't think so. I've been watching you, you know. A girl has to be careful who she trusts." Gail smiled, turned around, and slid down in her seat, a ribbon of smoke rising over her head.

Not that I wouldn't like to, Nicole added silently.

But who could she tell? She couldn't tell anyone in their family unless she wanted Gail to be locked up for life. She couldn't tell Mr. Roarke—if their boss ever found out about Gail stealing food, he would fire her for sure. And Nicole had eaten that stolen food. They could *both* lose their jobs!

Not that Nicole wanted hers, but she didn't want to lose it in disgrace, either.

143

If I ever got fired for stealing . . .

She couldn't even finish that sentence.

Okay, where is he?

Melanie scanned the packed stands inside the CCHS gymnasium. At the Eight Prime meeting the night before, she'd overheard Jesse and Miguel discussing the fact that they planned to be at that night's basketball game. *So where the heck is he?*

"Go Wildcat Spirit!" Vanessa hollered, snapping Melanie back to reality. She was supposed to be cheering, not mooning over Jesse.

She lined up with the rest of the squad, her movements crisp and sharp as Vanessa led the cheer. As many times as Sandra had made them practice it, Melanie felt like she could do that routine in her sleep. She could even do it with one eye on the stands, she discovered, starting her search afresh.

I'll just do this row by row, she decided, completely oblivious to the squad cheering around her, the basketball game being fought behind her, and more than ninety-five percent of the crowd in the stands. The only people who existed for her were tall teenage guys with short brown hair, wearing green lettermen's jackets.

None in the back row. She dropped her eyes slightly and started on the next row, scanning left to right as if reading a book.

The cheer came to an end. The rest of the cheerleaders finished off with a signature jump or a couple of kicks, then turned back toward the action on the polished wood floor. But Melanie kept her body sideways, her eyes still scanning the crowd.

Seeing Jesse at his house the night before had really made up her mind. She thought she'd been sure before, but now every day they weren't together was just a wasted opportunity—and Melanie didn't plan to waste any more. There was no way Jesse was leaving that gym without her.

If we win, The Danger Zone will be packed, she thought, still scanning. *That would be the perfect place to show up and let everyone see us together.*

Although there wouldn't be lots of privacy.

Maybe it would be better to go somewhere quieter, she decided grudgingly. As much as she couldn't wait to flaunt Jesse in Vanessa's face, she needed to be sure the two of them were solid first.

A trip to the lake ought to cement things. Her heart fluttered as she imagined the water glowing under the winter moonlight, Jesse's warm BMW the only spot of color in an otherwise silvered landscape. His arms would hold her tight again. They could say everything they felt and then—

There he is!

About six rows from the top and all the way to the right, Jesse was barely visible on the far side of a girl with dark, curly hair. Melanie focused on him, just able to make out a slice of his profile. Suddenly, as if feeling her eyes upon him, Jesse turned his head and looked right at her. Electricity arced between them. He leaned toward her slightly, more into her view.

Then he put his arm around the dark-haired girl beside him. He did it slowly, deliberately. His eyes never left Melanie's as he pulled the stranger close to his side and buried his chin in her curls.

Is he messing with me? she thought, her heart pounding from the shock. *Is he trying to make me jealous?*

Or had he already moved on, just like she'd predicted he would?

A loud squealing of sneakers on the wood floor beside her made Melanie turn her head only an instant before a body slammed into hers. The impact was bone-jarring, and the whole thing happened so quickly she didn't even have time to put out her hands to break her fall. Melanie crashed to the boards, a sweaty Ricky Black sprawled half on top of her. The crowd oohed as the pair went down but cheered with relief a moment later when Ricky jumped to his feet.

"Gee, Melanie, I'd be *happy* to go out with you," he teased, reaching down to help her up. "You don't have to throw yourself at me."

He ran back onto the court, his hands raised to the crowd. "She wants me!" he shouted to roars of laughter.

"Are you okay?" Tanya Jeffries rushed over as Melanie checked herself for bruises. All the other

146

cheerleaders crowded around too, to make sure she was all right.

"Yes, fine," Melanie said quickly.

"You're supposed to be watching the game, not the stands," Vanessa told her. "If you'd had your eyes on the ball that never would have happened."

"I know," Melanie admitted, rendering her captain speechless.

She could feel her cheeks burning, but not from the embarrassment of being knocked flat in front of all those people. Not even from having to acknowledge that Vanessa was right.

She didn't dare look at Jesse again.

If he was serious about that girl he was with, then getting knocked on her butt was the least part of how foolish she felt.

"Do you want to go to The Danger Zone?" Miguel asked, opening his passenger door for Leah.

"Not really."

In fact, the last thing she wanted to do on this precious rare date with Miguel was spend the rest of it in a dark, noisy arcade, fighting the crowd just to order a soda. It was bad enough that they'd already wasted most of the night watching a game she wasn't interested in, sitting cheek by jowl with Peter and Jenna.

"Let's park somewhere," she said impulsively.

147

Miguel seemed taken aback, but a moment later he smiled with a trace of his old mischief. "What's wrong with right here?"

They had arrived at the game too late to find a spot next to the gym and had ended up on the fringes of the more distant student parking lot. Now the few cars that remained were mostly rolling toward the exits, and Miguel's was left by itself in the shadows. Still . . .

"It's not exactly romantic."

Miguel's grin only grew broader. "It will be when the windows steam up."

Leah found herself smiling as well. "Well, if you're going to sweet-talk me like that," she said, moving into his arms.

But their kisses were tentative, their embraces clumsy. With everything that had happened between them, Leah wanted so badly to make every kiss count that she overthought each movement, as if she were taking a test. Miguel seemed rusty too, until he broke off to whisper in her ear.

"I love you, Leah. I really do."

"I love you, too," she answered, her heart in her throat. "So much."

Her arms tightened around him. She wanted to feel his heartbeat through her skin, to match her breathing to his. Their kisses grew hungrier, more intense. The passion inside the car rose until Leah felt it spread through every cell of her body. She clung to

148

him, her sense of the inevitable growing stronger by the second.

She loved him. He loved her. Wasn't everything else just details?

"I *do* want to marry you, Miguel," she said, giving in to her feelings. "I do. Yes."

Twelve

Melanie had just reached the base of the Andrewses' curving staircase on her way from her bedroom to the kitchen when the Saturday-morning mail dropped through the slot in her front door.

She almost walked right by it. For one thing, the mail was usually nothing but bills. For another, she was so stiff and bruised from her collision with Ricky Black the night before that every extra step was agony. But the biggest reason was that she simply didn't have the energy even to hope for a letter.

After spotting Jesse with that girl the night before, she'd had to put every bit of her willpower into faking her brightest smiles for the rest of the game. And she'd learned that she wasn't as good an actress as she'd once been. Her cheeks had felt as if they were going to crack the entire evening—and she'd been sure the cracks were showing. The moment the postgame cheers were over, Melanie had persuaded Tanya to drop her off at home, declining every invitation to join the crowd at The Danger Zone.

Now, twelve hours later, she had the worst type of

hangover—the type produced by too many tears. Her head throbbed with a pressure that buzzed in her ears, her stomach felt queasy and tight, and her red eyes were swollen scratchy. And, exactly like a person who had overindulged in alcohol, she regretted her excesses in the worst way. There was no doubt in her mind now that she had made a larger fool of herself than circumstances had dictated.

Why cry herself sick simply because Jesse had been seen with some random girl at the game? For all Melanie knew, that girl was a cousin or something.

Well, probably not, she thought, deciding to check out the mail after all. Jesse's family was from California, and Melanie was sure that if there were any stray cousins scattered around Missouri she'd have heard about them by now.

But even so, she was crazy to assume that girl was someone important. For all she knew, Jesse was just trying to make her jealous—and there was a big part of her that had realized as much the night before. Even as she'd been sobbing her eyes out, she'd known it might be for no reason.

Except that now, in the cold light of day, she had to admit that it wasn't just Jesse she'd been crying about. And it wasn't the embarrassment of being flattened in front of the home crowd. *And it sure wasn't a couple of stupid bruises,* she thought as the tears welled into her eyes again. It was just . . .

Everything.

Picking the mail up off the floor, she immediately noticed a stiff white card, addressed to her in bold handwriting. She checked the return address—the card was from Aunt Gwen, her mother's only sibling.

Melanie sucked in her breath. Why was Aunt Gwen writing to her? Why now? They had never been close, and they hadn't spoken once since Melanie's mother had died.

For a long time, Melanie had been furious with her aunt for sending an announcement for her mother's funeral, certain Gwen was paying her back for not attending the services. Melanie's grief had been too raw back then, her loss too unexpected. And her pain had only been compounded by her certainty that there was nothing after death but decay. With that belief, or lack thereof, a funeral was at best a hollow event, and she hadn't wanted to go.

The fact that her mother had been buried in Iowa, where the rest of her family still lived, hadn't helped. Melanie had been thirteen years old then; it wasn't as if she could change her mind at the last minute and drive on up. At the time, the funeral announcement had been nothing but salt in her wounds. But now—now that she'd used the map on the back to visit her mother's grave—she thought she finally understood what her aunt had been thinking.

She wanted me to know where it was. Just in case . . .

Popping the seal on the flap of the envelope,

Melanie took out the card. THINKING OF YOU, it said on the front, the words underlining a generic winter scene.

Melanie snorted involuntarily, her defenses on red alert. Her pulse raced with the fear of being hurt by her family again as she slowly opened the card.

Dear Melanie,

It has been a long time since I've written, but I think about you often. I hope you are well and happy, and that you're enjoying high school. We are all fine here, although your grandparents find these cold winters tougher and tougher to get through.

I am writing to let you know how much I would love to see you. I won't pretend the past didn't happen, but perhaps old hurts have healed enough that we could all start fresh. I always regretted the fight that kept us from visiting Tristyn after she married, and that kept me from knowing you. But I am your only aunt, you are my only niece, and I would like more than anything to put things right between us.

It occurred to me that you might like to visit here sometime. I could show you the town where your mother grew up, and all her favorite places. I know how it must seem to you, but there isn't just death here, Melanie. Your mom had a beautiful life here too.

I live by myself these days, and I have a spare room you'd be welcome to stay in as long as you like—although you may have to convince an old cat to sleep somewhere else. If you think you'd like to come, I'd be happy to drive down and pick you up. Please write back and let me know. You truly are

Always in my heart,
Aunt Gwen

Melanie stared at the card in her hands. Was this woman, a virtual stranger, seriously proposing that Melanie be her houseguest? Why?

Like I'd really go. She's nuts!

Although she couldn't deny a certain curiosity. Just the fact that her aunt had invited her had Melanie's imagination racing a dozen different ways. Still, the bad feelings she held toward the rest of her family ran much deeper than idle interest.

Dad would have a conniption, she thought, resuming her slow, painful limp to the kitchen. Aunt Gwen was either really brave or really stupid to put her return address on that envelope. If he had picked up the mail . . .

Luckily he hadn't, and Melanie didn't plan to mention the card. She wasn't in the mood for the drama, for one thing. More importantly, why bother?

She had absolutely no intention of ever writing back. And as far as actually going to Iowa . . .

Yeah, right, she thought, shaking her aching head.

* * *

154

"Let me help you," Jenna pleaded, following her older sister through the house.

Caitlin had just arrived home from her first round of Saturday-morning dog walking, and Jenna knew her sister would hang around the kitchen barely long enough to warm up and drink something hot before she took off again.

Reaching the kitchen, Caitlin put a coffee mug of water in the microwave to heat. "I don't need any help, Jenna. I'm almost done."

"You're *not* almost done. Besides, if I come along we can take care of Sunday's dogs today. Think how happy that would make Mom."

"I can't walk Sunday's dogs today, because those are *Sunday's* dogs. I have a schedule, Jenna, and I can't just change it on the spur of the moment. People are counting on me to be there at certain times."

"What if you called them first?"

"What for? I'm perfectly on schedule now, and I'll be ready for the early service tomorrow."

"All right!" Jenna said, throwing up her hands. "I admit it—I have no good reason at all. Just let me go with you, Caitlin. I miss hanging out with you."

Caitlin bobbed a tea bag up and down in her mug. "You could have said that in the first place."

"Would it have worked?"

"Probably not." But a smile flicked across Caitlin's lips.

Jenna grabbed at that straw. "Okay, so I'm going. Right?"

"If you have to."

"I do! I really do."

The two girls walked dogs for hours that day. At first Caitlin met most of Jenna's attempts to start a conversation with shrugs or shakes of her head. But as the morning wore on, the sun came out in a welcome way, seeming to work its thaw on Caitlin as much as on the cold ground. She gradually began talking, first to the dogs, then finally to Jenna.

"Do you know what Dr. Campbell is going to let me do next week?" Caitlin asked when the sisters were down to their last two dogs. Jenna was walking a greyhound named Whizzer; Caitlin, a large, mostly tan mixed-breed.

"No. What?"

"I'm going to learn to prep the animals for surgery. You know, shave the surgery area and disinfect it and all that."

"That's great, Caitlin! Are you excited?"

"Of course."

"Next you'll be wanting to do the surgery too."

"I wish I could, but you have to go to veterinary school for that. It seems like such a waste when I could just learn by watching Dr. Campbell."

Jenna was taken aback. "Well, of course you'd have to go to school. You wouldn't want *your* doctor to learn just by watching."

Caitlin shrugged. "I'll bet that's how they did it in the old days."

"Maybe," Jenna said slowly. She'd never really thought about it before. "Anyway, I'm sure Dr. Campbell will let you do as much as you're allowed to."

"Yes," Caitlin confirmed, nodding happily. "Hey, turn here and we'll take Whizzer home the back way."

Jenna guided the high-spirited greyhound around the corner, feeling like she was finally getting the hang of it. If Whizzer still didn't trot at her heels, at least he knew who was boss now. They dropped him off at his small house, his gray-haired owner grateful as she accepted the big dog's leash.

"You always wear him out so nicely, Caitlin," she said with a smile. "I don't know what we'd do without you. Isn't that right, Bizzywizz?"

Whizzer wagged, and Caitlin blushed. "Thanks, Mrs. MacGregor. We'll see you tomorrow, all right?"

As they walked down the front path out to the street, Jenna tried to take the leash of the last remaining dog. "Let me walk Molly now. Give your arms a break."

Caitlin waved her away. "Are you kidding? Molly's a sweetheart—no trouble at all."

"She pulls that leash pretty good."

"She's just happy. Aren't you, Molly?" Caitlin asked, reaching forward to pat the dog's back. Molly turned her head and licked Caitlin's hand before straining forward again.

"Caitlin," Jenna said impulsively, touching her sister on the shoulder. "I really *was* only trying to help you when I blabbed to Peter about David. I know I shouldn't have done it, though, and I'm really, *really* sorry. Are we okay now? You and I, I mean."

"Peter hasn't said anything to David?" Caitlin asked tensely.

"No! Not a word!" Jenna promised, grateful almost to tears that she had called off that plan.

Caitlin took a minute before she answered. "I guess so."

It wasn't the most enthusiastic reply, nor was it the "yes" Jenna had hoped for. But it was a place to start.

"I'm so glad," she said as she tagged along at her sister's side. "And I'm going to make it up to you, I promise."

Caitlin raised her brows. "If you want to make it up to me, stay out of my private life."

"Right," Jenna said quickly. "That's exactly what I meant."

It was now, anyway.

"All right," Nicole said dubiously, jotting down the address. "If it's okay with my parents, I guess I'll see you there." She hung up the phone just as her mother walked into the kitchen.

"Who was that?" Mrs. Brewster asked irritably. "I hate the way your friends always call so close to dinner."

"You haven't even started dinner yet," Nicole pointed out, barely caring if her mom got angry. "Besides, it wasn't one of my friends. It was Gail."

"Gail!" Mrs. Brewster cried, her sour expression sweetening. "What did she want?"

"She called to invite me to a Mapleton party tonight. I told her I thought I could go, but if you don't want me to I'll—"

"A party with Gail? Of course you can go!" said her mother. "In fact, I can't think of anyone I'd rather have you go out with."

If you only knew, Nicole thought, remembering the scene in Neil's Camaro the night before.

"I guess I'll go, then," she said sullenly.

"By all means! Do you need my car?"

"I do, actually." Knowing what she did now, there was no way Nicole wanted to depend on either Neil or Gail for a ride at the end of a party. "And I might be home a little late."

"That's all right," Mrs. Brewster said magnanimously. "I don't think we need to worry about curfew when you're out with someone so responsible."

Right, thought Nicole, forcing a smile. *You just keep thinking that.*

"What are you going to wear?"

"I, uh—I'd better go figure that out." Retreating from the kitchen, Nicole ran upstairs to her room.

"Great," she groaned as the door closed behind her. "Just what I want to do."

The only reason she hadn't told Gail no the instant the party was mentioned was that she knew Courtney wouldn't be calling with a better offer, or calling at all, for that matter—*not* that Nicole cared. Besides, she didn't want her cousin to think she was uncool. Nicole could party with the best of them—wasn't that how she'd been forced into that stupid job at Wienerageous in the first place?—and before she could argue Gail to her senses, she needed to prove she was as normal as anyone else.

And Nicole *definitely* planned to argue Gail to her senses. Forget making fun of their boss, forget her questionable wisdom in dating Neil, forget even the clear idiocy of the cigarettes—those things could stay Gail's business. But the stealing had to stop. Not only was it was wrong, it was likely to get them both in trouble.

I'm going to have to talk to her, Nicole thought, flipping distractedly through the clothes in her closet. *And tonight's as good a time as any.*

It was the only good thing about having to go to the party, really.

It's safer than trying to talk at work, she thought,

yanking a top off its hanger. *And it's smarter to do it now, before both our rears end up in a sling.*

She pulled down a sweater to add to the shirt.

But what if she doesn't listen? a little voice asked.

Nicole drew a deep, nervous breath, then headed for her dresser. *She will,* she thought determinedly. *She'd better.*

Thirteen

"May I bring you a wine list, sir?" the waiter asked as he showed Miguel and Leah to a quiet corner of the fancy French restaurant.

Miguel hesitated with his answer as he pulled Leah's chair out for her. They ought to have champagne for such an important occasion, but if the waiter asked for ID and learned they were only seventeen it would be pretty embarrassing.

"Leah?" Miguel asked.

"Not for me, thanks," she responded quickly, shaking her head as he took the chair across from hers.

Not worth it, her expression signaled. *Don't try.*

"No, thank you," Miguel told the waiter.

The man nodded respectfully and walked off, but Miguel couldn't help seeing the entire encounter as a bad sign. He and Leah weren't even old enough to order a glass of wine. What were they doing cementing an engagement?

There's got to be something wrong with a law that lets people get married before they can drink, he thought distractedly, staring at Leah.

She looked absolutely beautiful that night, with her hair pinned up and more makeup on than usual. They had both dressed as formally as they'd dared, wanting to honor the specialness of the occasion, but because they'd agreed to keep their engagement to themselves a little longer, they'd had to stay casual enough to avoid arousing their parents' suspicions. Miguel would have loved to see her wear the fancy sequined gown she'd competed in at the U.S. Girls contest, but Leah had balked at that suggestion as guaranteed to tip her parents off. Instead she was wearing an everyday dress he'd seen before—pretty, but not too exciting.

He sighed. The dress didn't really matter, but the compromise bothered him. Ever since they'd begun considering marriage, it seemed like compromise was all they did.

"This place is fancy!" Leah said, opening her menu. "What are you going to have?"

"Huh? Oh." Miguel opened his menu too. "I don't know. This stuff is all in French."

Leah laughed. "Amazingly enough."

But she seemed restless as her eyes scanned the selections, and he wondered if her mind was as full of questions and doubts as his own.

The waiter returned and took their orders, leaving behind a basket of bread. Leah tore the crust off a still-warm roll and toyed with the star-shaped pats of butter in the china butter dish.

"So, did you, uh, give any more thought to my idea for our wedding?" she asked.

"You mean the lake?"

The night before, in his car, Leah had proposed holding an outdoor ceremony on the long, jutting rock where they had first kissed. It wasn't what he'd had in mind, but under the circumstances, maybe it was the best compromise.

"If that's what you want, I guess it will be all right."

Leah frowned slightly. "It'll be more than all right—it'll be romantic."

"I know."

If Leah was willing to marry him on a rock, how could he complain about the loss of his big church wedding? Anyway, girls were the ones who were supposed to care about things like that, not guys.

"When do you want to do it?" Leah asked.

"You want to pick a date now?"

"Well, let's pick a month, at least." Leah put down her bread, no longer even pretending to find it interesting. "September or October would be best, I think. June doesn't give us enough time after graduation, and July and August are too hot."

"If we wait until fall, we'll have a lot fewer guests. Everyone who graduates this year will have already gone off to college."

Leah flinched at the mention of college, and he could only imagine what she was thinking. Instead of pursuing that discussion, however, she quickly changed the subject.

"We'll have to get an apartment," she said. "Houses are too expensive."

The idea that Leah thought she could tell him anything about economizing almost made him laugh. "You're right," he managed to say somehow.

The waiter appeared with the food. Miguel dug in without even seeing it, his mind on the pressing question of rent. He'd already looked in the newspaper, and he and Leah were going to have to rent a studio, or a one-bedroom at the most.

Once he graduated, he'd make pretty decent money working full-time for Mr. Ambrosi, but it was a mystery to him how Leah would earn more than minimum wage. Miguel felt lucky to have job experience, but Leah had never worked. With no experience and no degree, he was afraid she was going to have a hard time finding anything that didn't bore her to tears. But she was going to have to work anyway—they were going to need her income.

"I still want to get my mom her own place," he blurted out. "I know we'll be married, and she's pretty well now, but I've got to get her out of public housing. I said I would and I will."

Leah looked up from her plate. "All right."

"And we're going to have to get her a car. I'd give her mine, but it's too junky."

"It's good enough for us, though," Leah interpreted. She didn't look pleased by the idea.

"At least I can fix it when it breaks down."

"We're going to need a car for me, too."

"What? Why?"

"I'm going to be working, Miguel. I'm going to be *married*. If I'm going to be dependent on you to borrow the car, I might as well stay at home with my parents."

"Oh."

Miguel kept eating, but the expensive food seemed tasteless. Just when he'd thought he was about to get his family out of debt, debt was all he could see in front of him for the next ten years. Forget about college, forget about his recent dream of becoming a doctor, *really* forget about Europe—he and Leah would be lucky if they could afford to honeymoon in Mapleton. They weren't going to want to live in an apartment forever, and houses cost a lot of money. And if they were ever to have kids . . .

Miguel put down his fork. Kids would be a life sentence.

For the first time he understood—really understood—what had happened to his father: married too young, kids almost immediately, working every minute just to give his family a decent life, dying in debt.

And it wasn't as if the whole affair had been a picnic for his mother, either.

What are we doing? he worried, completely forgetting he ought to be happy. He was in such a sweat of second thoughts he felt sick.

As if reading his mind, Leah reached across the table and put one of her hands over his.

"You *do* still want to do this. Right?"

Miguel took a deep breath. "Of course. Don't you?"

"Gail!" Nicole whispered worriedly, hovering at her cousin's elbow. "Don't you think you've had enough?"

"I'm still standing, aren't I?"

Gail pulled another beer from the ice chest and stepped out of the crowded kitchen. She seemed pretty steady on her feet, but her words had the clipped precision of someone who was concentrating too hard, and her eyes were as glassy as marbles.

"How many is that?" asked Nicole.

"Why? Are you planning to outdrink me?"

"I just think you ought to slow down."

"Oh, come on, Nicole. I thought you were cool."

Nicole cast a nervous glance around the dark interior of the apartment where the party was being held. Of the thirty or so people there, she and Gail looked by far the youngest. Worse, everyone else was a total stranger. From what Nicole could gather, the group was composed primarily of Mapleton High School graduates—and more than a few dropouts. "Where's Neil?"

167

"Probably with Bill." Gail gave her a reproachful look as she twisted the cap off at least her sixth beer. "Which is where *you* ought to be. What's the matter? Don't you think he's cute?"

"Not exactly."

Aside from the fact that a fix-up was the last thing she'd expected, Nicole didn't plan to spend two minutes alone with Neil's friend Bill. The guy was skinny, scary, and, judging by his behavior, high on something other than beer.

"I wouldn't have invited you if I'd known you were going to be such dead weight," Gail declared, lighting another cigarette.

And I wouldn't have come if I'd known that talking to you would be such a waste of time, thought Nicole.

From the moment they'd arrived at the party, Gail had been completely out of control. Bouncing from hanging on Neil to sucking down beers, smoking the whole time, she'd brushed off every attempt at serious conversation by acting as if Nicole were less cool than she was. Taking a deep breath, Nicole decided to give it one last try.

"You know, Gail, everyone's luck runs out sooner or later. I'm no angel myself, but if you keep messing with Mr. Roarke—"

Gail staggered backward, her red-rimmed eyes horrified.

"Holy hot dogs, Bun Girl! This is a *party*. There's

168

got to be a law against talking about someone's boss at a party."

"Gail, I—"

"I'm not listening!" Gail sang, skipping off toward the living room.

Nicole sighed, then reluctantly followed her cousin into the heart of the crowd.

Compared to the open CCHS parties Nicole was used to, this one was small and relatively quiet. The stereo was on but not blaring, and no one was dancing—or doing much of anything besides drinking and smoking. The guests clustered in the kitchen, the living room, and the short passage in between, barely venturing anywhere else.

In the living room, the furniture was horrendously shabby, so much so that the bodies draped all over it represented an improvement. The people who couldn't find places spilled over onto the floor, sitting cross-legged on the crusty carpeting, surrounded by ashtrays and empty bottles. As far as Nicole could tell, the entire point of the gathering was to drink as much as possible; the music and conversation were simply there to fill the gaps between swallows.

Gail walked out to the center of the room and stood there, swaying slightly. "Where's Neil?" she asked anyone who was listening.

"He and Bill went out on a run, didn't they?" one of the guys answered.

The girl in his lap caught him with a back-jabbed elbow. "I don't think so," she said with a significant glance at Nicole.

Everyone else in the room seemed to catch her suspicion, turning cold eyes Nicole's way.

Don't worry, Nicole wanted to shout. *I don't know what you're talking about, and I don't want to know.*

Boy, did she not want to know.

Gail stepped forward and turned up the stereo, then began dancing by herself in the open center of the room. The song was fast, but Gail's movements were slow and seductive. Her eyes dropped closed as she felt her way along the beat, pausing only for regular sips from the bottle still clenched in one hand. Nicole watched her cousin in amazement, as mesmerized as the rest of the group.

She's wasted, Nicole thought. *She must be.*

Gail's behavior so far at this party was making Nicole's little screwup on New Year's Eve look like small potatoes. And Nicole didn't think the way some of the guys were starting to eye her cousin was such a good thing.

"Come on, Gail," she said tensely, stepping forward and grabbing one arm.

Gail's eyes flew open. "Hey, Nicole!" she said happily. "You want to dance?"

"No. No one else is dancing, Gail. And I think—"

"Neil!" Gail squealed, tearing free of Nicole to run to her boyfriend.

He and Bill had just come in the front door, letting a tiny breath of fresh air into the smoke-filled apartment. Bill stood leering at Nicole as Neil's hands roamed over Gail.

"Hey, babe. Did you miss me?"

"You should have told me you were going," Gail reproached him, pouting like a little girl. "Did you get what you wanted?"

Neil smiled. "I always get what I want, Jelly."

Not waiting to hear another word, Nicole rushed forward, took Gail by an arm, and pulled her off to one side of the room.

"Listen, Gail. I'm going home now, and I think you'd better let me drop you off first. Is there some way you can get to your room without your parents seeing you?"

If not, Nicole predicted big problems ahead, because there was no way she could take Gail home in her current condition.

"Don't worry about me," Gail said, leaning in way too close. Her breath reeked of beer and cigarettes. "I told my mother I was sleeping at your house tonight."

"At *my* house!" Nicole gasped. "If my mom sees you like this she'll flip!"

Gail made a face. "Don't be dense. I'm not *going* to your house, that's just our story. Right?"

"But if you're not going to my house and you're not going home . . ."

171

"Hel-*lo*. I have a boyfriend, in case you haven't noticed."

As if she had called his name, Neil chose that moment to walk up and slip his tattooed arms around Gail. "What's going on?"

Nicole's heart pounded as she realized what Gail was driving at. Not only was her cousin planning to stay out all night with her boyfriend, she intended to use Nicole as her cover. Worse, she was calling the whole thing "our" story. *If my mom ever finds out . . .*

I haven't done anything wrong, Nicole reassured herself quickly, taking a deep breath. *I haven't told any lies.*

But what would she say if Aunt Ellen called and Gail wasn't even there?

Fourteen

"I shouldn't have let you help me yesterday," Caitlin whispered guiltily as Jenna blew her nose again. "You sound like you have pneumonia."

"I'm fine," Jenna snuffled. "Just a little congested."

Caitlin nodded toward the front of the church, where the choir would be filing out any minute. "If Mom didn't let you sing, you must be closer to death than you think."

"I'm fine," Jenna repeated. "Besides, it was worth it."

It was more than worth it, actually. Not only were Caitlin's dogs all walked, leaving Caitlin free to come to the early service with the family, but that morning she had finally taken the ribbon off the Fire & Water T-shirt Jenna had brought her and put it away in her dresser. True, she hadn't worn it, but even getting her to look at it was progress.

"I hope you don't miss school tomorrow," Caitlin said.

Down at the end of the pew, Maggie and Allison started giggling about some private joke, which

Sarah begged to be let in on. Mr. Conrad hushed them all and Jenna turned her head to add her own disapproving stare. She was still looking in that direction when Peter appeared in the aisle, walking side by side with David.

David?

Jenna stiffened in the pew, her heart pounding. *What is David doing in Clearwater Crossing? Why isn't he at school? Why didn't Peter call me?*

Without taking her eyes off the brothers, Jenna reached behind her to squeeze Caitlin's knee. "Look!" she whispered through clenched teeth. "Look who's here!"

"I see," Caitlin whispered back, loosening Jenna's fingers.

Jenna waved at Peter and David, then watched as they chose seats near the front of the church. If only there had been room left next to her and Caitlin! But their pew was full, as was most of the church, and the service was due to begin any second. There was no time for musical chairs. As if to underscore that point, the choir filed out and began the first hymn.

This is going to kill me! Jenna thought, croaking along with the song as she looked back and forth from David to Caitlin. Her sister's cheeks were flushed, her eyes lowered to the pages of a hymnal Jenna knew she didn't need. *How can Caitlin act so cool?*

All through the service, Jenna fidgeted in her seat. Reverend Thompson's sermon was lost to her that day, coming through in disjointed snatches as she stared at the back of David's blond head. There was no telling what he was doing there, but there was also no disputing that Mary Beth was all the way off in Nashville. The moment the final hymn was sung, Jenna turned to Caitlin.

"This is your big chance!" she hissed as the congregation rose and people began walking out. "You have to go talk to him!"

The younger Conrad girls began filing into the aisle with their father, but Caitlin hesitated, looking doubtfully in David's direction. As desperately as Jenna wanted her sister to march over there and ask him what was going on, she had a sinking feeling it would never happen.

Then a better idea occurred to her. "Come on," she said. "I think I know another way."

Moving out into the traffic headed for the main door, Jenna crawled impatiently along with the crowd, glancing back over her shoulder every couple of seconds to make sure Caitlin was still right behind her. At last they reached the broad steps outside, then the pavement. The area was awash in winter sunshine, making Jenna's favorite bench at the edge of the landscaping the perfect place to wait. She and Peter usually met at the bench after every service anyway, so there would be nothing unusual about her and Caitlin hanging out there. And if Peter had the sense she gave him credit for . . .

Don't let me down, Peter, she thought, hoping he'd catch her vibe somehow.

Saying she wasn't going to interfere in Caitlin's life was all well and good when David was out of town. But now that Caitlin and her crush were within spitting distance of each other, all previous resolutions were off. Peter *had* to bring David out to talk to Caitlin. He just had to.

A few minutes later, the pair showed up.

"Hi, Jenna!" Peter said cheerily. "How come you weren't singing?"

"I have a cold, but I'm fine," she answered, turning her attention to his brother. "I'm really surprised to see *you* here, David. Is there a college holiday? Because if there is, Mary Beth doesn't have it—she's still at school."

Maybe it wasn't the most subtle approach, but it got her point across.

"No. No holiday. I've been studying hard the last few weekends, though, and I'm so caught up that I decided to take Monday off and come home for a couple of days."

"He just got here this morning," Peter added quickly. "We were *all* really surprised."

Okay, so he knows he should have called me, Jenna thought.

"And you're going back tomorrow?" she asked David.

David shrugged. "That's the plan."

Caitlin still hadn't said a word. Jenna was trying to figure out how to draw her into the conversation when Peter interrupted her scheming.

"Hey, Jenna, where's your dad? I want to ask him something."

"Ask him what?" Jenna said, shaking her head to discourage him. No way was she leaving Caitlin's side just when things were getting interesting.

"I want to know what kind of film he used in the camera when he took our Christmas picture."

"You *what*?"

But Peter had grabbed her hand and was already pulling her back toward the front of the church, away from Caitlin and David.

"What are you doing?" she whispered frantically as he towed her across the pavement. "Are you crazy? Now we don't know what's going on."

Peter smiled. "Probably nothing. But you can be sure it would have been nothing as long as we were standing there listening."

"Oh. Right."

She hated to admit it, but Peter had a point. She let him lead her to the bottom of the steps, where her father and younger sisters were hanging out talking to friends. Instead of joining their group, however, Jenna hung back on the fringes, surreptitiously watching Caitlin and David.

"I wonder what they're talking about," she said, squeezing Peter's hand. "Did David tell you why he's really here?"

"No."

Jenna felt ready to burst with her questions as she looked back toward the bench, hoping for a clue. The pair was carrying on a conversation now, although Caitlin was still spending more time watching her shoes than David's face.

Please, please, please let this go well for her, Jenna prayed, squeezing her eyes shut.

"I just remembered," Peter said. "David's got the car keys. If he and Caitlin take off together, can I bum a ride home with you guys?"

Jenna's eyes flew open. "You don't really think that will happen?"

Peter shrugged and nodded toward the parking lot. "Looks like it's happening already."

Jenna whipped her head around, astonished to see Caitlin and David walking toward the Altmanns' Toyota.

"I can't believe she's just leaving like that, without telling Dad or anything!"

"I'm sure she knows you're watching, and you can tell him for her."

"That's right," Jenna agreed, nodding distractedly. "That's right, I can."

Caitlin and David climbed into the car and

closed the doors. Jenna's heart was thumping as she watched them drive away.

Oh please, oh please, oh please, she thought, crossing her fingers.

"So how about it?" Peter asked. "Is it okay if I ride home with you?"

"Are you kidding?" She'd have volunteered to carry him home on her back if she'd known it meant Caitlin and David would have a car to themselves.

"Do you think he likes her?" she blurted out.

"I honestly don't know."

"Did you say anything to him about how Caitlin feels?"

"No."

"Ohhh," Jenna groaned. "How am I going to stand it until Caitlin gets home and tells me what's happening?"

Then a horrible second thought struck her: Caitlin *would* tell her what was happening.

Wouldn't she?

"Mom, you're happy with Dad, right?" Leah asked.

Mrs. Rosenthal put down the Sunday paper and peered at Leah over her coffee cup. "Of course. What makes you ask that?"

"Nothing," Leah said untruthfully, her mind consumed with thoughts of marrying Miguel. "It just seems like a lot of people are getting divorced these days."

Leah's mother relaxed. "A lot of people get married who have no business even thinking about it. Don't worry about me and your father, though. We waited until we were sure we knew what we were getting into."

"Five years, right?" Leah had heard the story many times before—how her parents had waited until they were both not only out of college but also established in their careers—but she suddenly felt the need to hear it once again.

"Five years from the point we knew we wanted to marry. It was more like eight years from the time we met."

Eight years! Leah hadn't remembered that part, and her mind boggled at the information. She'd known Miguel less than five months.

"Do you really think you needed to wait so long?"

Mrs. Rosenthal nodded. "We did. Absolutely. Being married's not always easy, you know, and it seems to me that people make two main mistakes. The big one is choosing the wrong partner. There's no recovering from that one, so all I can say is, make sure you're choosing with both eyes open."

"What's the second one?" Leah asked. Her voice sounded a little breathless, but her mother didn't seem to notice.

"Huh? Oh. That would be getting married without a decent income. Money isn't everything, but it starts to feel that way when you don't have any. If people have to give up enough of their dreams just to pay the rent, they start to resent the whole situation."

She paused to sip her coffee. "Choosing right, though. That's the main thing. If two people are just incompatible, there's nothing in this world that can save them."

"I guess you and Dad must be about the most compatible two people in the world," Leah said, her anxiety growing by the second. "You like all the same things. You even have the same job."

"It's nice to have things in common, but compatibility goes a lot deeper than that. You need to have the same goals, the same values. You need to react the same way in a crisis. And it's a big plus if you both believe the same things. I remember when your father and I first got engaged, your grandmother Rosenthal . . . well . . . never mind. In-laws are a whole different topic."

Her mother frowned, then shook it off. "Why are we even talking about this? You don't need to be thinking about marriage for at least five years. Hopefully more like ten."

"Right," Leah said uneasily.

Mrs. Rosenthal seemed to catch something in her daughter's tone. "You *aren't* thinking about marriage," she said, watching Leah closely.

Leah's pulse raced until it felt as if her heart would beat out of her chest. She and Miguel hadn't planned to tell their parents about their engagement for at least another week, and she wanted him to be there when she broke the big news.

"No, I'm not thinking about it," Leah said, trying to keep her gaze level as she got up from the table.

"That's good," said her mother, returning to the paper. "Boy, you had me going there for a minute!"

Leah did her best to smile before she turned and headed for her room.

I'm not thinking about it, she repeated silently as she walked. *Because I already thought about it and now I've decided to do it.*

But no amount of rationalizing was going to make her feel better about the way she had just deceived her mother. She was sick at heart as she opened her bedroom door, worried about how she'd break the news when that day finally arrived.

Or maybe it was the news itself she was worried about. Her little talk with her mom hadn't exactly boosted her confidence.

I should be happy. No, I should be ecstatic.

So how come she couldn't help worrying that she and Miguel were making the biggest mistake of their lives?

Nicole strained forward in her pew, hanging on Pastor Ramsey's words. Normally she barely paid attention to his sermons—his points tended to ramble all over the place, and his old voice was sleep-inducing—but that day she was desperate for guidance. If the pastor had any information that could shed some light on her problems with Gail, she definitely wanted to hear it. Nicole's open Bible lay forgotten on her lap, and she was hardly aware of her parents in the seats to her right or the other people all around her as she filtered every word, trying to make them fit her current situation.

There was no doubt in Nicole's mind that she was in a major moral dilemma. Gail was in trouble, and the way things were headed she was sure to be in even bigger trouble soon. To Nicole's amazement, though, she no longer wanted to see her perfect cousin fall off her pedestal; she wanted her to shape up.

But what could Nicole do? If she told on Gail, she could say good-bye to any chance of remaining friends with her—not to mention how immature she'd look. On the other hand, all Nicole's efforts to persuade Gail herself had gone nowhere. At the party the night before, she had ended up fleeing, leaving Gail on her own. Nicole had tossed and turned all night, waiting for the inevitable phone call—from Aunt Ellen, from Mr. Roarke, from the police . . .

This morning her fears seemed a little ridiculous. Still, if Gail didn't turn things around, sooner or later that phone call *would* come. And in the chaos that ensued, Nicole would have to admit she'd known what Gail was doing all along. They'd *both* be in trouble then—and Nicole didn't even want to imagine how much.

She tried that much harder to focus on Pastor Ramsey. He was talking about Jonah and a big fish and Nineveh and a withering vine. Nicole heaved a sigh, not getting it. It made a good story, but what did it have to do with *her*?

Giving up, she closed her eyes and blocked out the pastor's voice.

Dear God, she prayed, *I could really use some help here.*

She paused a minute, not knowing what else to say. *And I really hope you're listening.*

Fifteen

Melanie chewed the inside of her lip as she waited beside Jesse's BMW after school on Monday. Although she'd spotted him in the cafeteria during lunch, she still hadn't spoken to him since she'd seen him with that girl at the Friday game. It had taken her all weekend to make up her mind to talk to him, but she'd finally decided to give it a try—and this time she was determined to make him listen.

If he knew how I really felt, he'd have to give me a chance, she thought nervously. *Unless he was lying about his feelings for me.*

Considering that she was dealing with Jesse, she wasn't prepared to rule anything out. But she'd seen his face when she'd broken up with him, and she still believed his distress had been genuine.

Taking a deep breath, she fussed with the buttons of her red coat. She would have liked to leave the coat open, to show off her new sweater, but the sunshine that had warmed the town the last two days still wasn't warm enough for that.

Jesse finally appeared on the school's front lawn, his head a little higher than the ones around him as he walked toward the parking lot. It wasn't until he got to the edge of the pavement, however, and most of the crowd had cleared out between them, that Melanie realized he was with someone—and this time she knew who it was. Brooke Henderson, the senior class president and homecoming queen, walked at Jesse's side, smiling at him as if smitten.

Brooke Henderson! Melanie thought. *She's dating Jon Young!*

So what was she doing with Jesse?

He's probably just giving her a ride.

Even so, Melanie didn't want to be anywhere in the vicinity when the two of them got to the car. Her eyes still on Jesse, Melanie began backing up, planning to lose herself in the parking lot. She had taken no more than a couple of steps, however, when Jesse looked right at her.

She froze, frantically trying to devise an escape plan. There was no way she wanted to talk to him in front of Brooke, but if she left now he would know she was running away.

Better to bluff it out, she decided, taking a deep breath.

Melanie kept her gaze steady as Jesse walked to the car. He stared her down in return, his face a practiced blank. Brooke, on the other hand, seemed oblivious to Melanie's presence as she chattered and laughed her way across the parking lot, intent on telling some story. She kept it up until the very last moment, when the three of them stood face-to-face.

"Oh. Hello, Melanie," she said cheerfully.

Melanie didn't know Brooke, but she was glad the older girl had decided not to play games. It would have been pretty silly for the homecoming queen and the school's only sophomore cheerleader to pretend not to recognize each other.

"Hello, Brooke."

"What do you want?" Jesse asked, his tone so rude that both girls stared.

"Well, I, uh . . . I just thought—" Melanie stammered.

"You thought I'd drive you home?" Jesse supplied.

That seemed like as good an excuse as any. "If you're already busy it's no big deal. I'll just take the bus."

"Gee, I'd really love to be your chauffeur, Melanie. *Again*," he added caustically. "But as you can see, I *am* kind of busy."

"I don't mind dropping Melanie—" Brooke began.

"I mind," Jesse said flatly.

Brooke shot her an apologetic glance, but Melanie couldn't even look at her. Not trusting her voice, to say good-bye, she spun blindly around and hurried toward the bus stop, blinking back tears as she went. She wouldn't let Brooke see her cry. She *certainly* wouldn't give Jesse that satisfaction.

But once she was safely in a back seat of the bus, her face hidden in her coat, the tears rained down her cheeks. Had she been completely deluded to think Jesse liked her? Anyone who had seen the way he'd just treated her would assume he couldn't even stand to have her around.

He hates me, she thought, sobbing into her lapel.

It didn't even matter anymore whether or not he liked Brooke, or who that girl at the game had been. Neither one of them was her, and Melanie was sure that was the message Jesse was trying to send.

The game was over. She was out.

When the bus let her off at her stop, she could barely maintain her dignity long enough to see it out of sight before she ran down the private road to her house and flew up the stairs to her room.

Nothing ever goes right for me, she thought hopelessly, slamming the door behind her. *Why didn't I make up my mind about Jesse until it was too late?*

A sudden longing to cry on Peter's shoulder seized her. How she missed him and the talks they used to have! But Peter was so wrapped up with Jenna these days, Melanie felt he'd all but abandoned her.

Throwing her coat on the floor, she walked into her huge closet and opened the drawer where she'd hidden the picture of her and Peter at the homecoming dance. Her fingers searched out the cardboard photographer's frame and opened it slowly, a hundred conflicting emotions racing through her.

If things had gone differently with Peter that night, she'd never have become involved with Jesse. She studied his face in the photograph now, so sure of himself, so at peace—a stark contrast to her own phony smile. How she envied him! He had no idea what it was like to be her, tossed every which way by her own doubts. When it came to the things that mattered, Peter had no doubt at all.

Sighing, she closed the frame and slipped it back under the lingerie in the drawer. But as she did her fingers came in contact with another hidden item— the greeting card from Aunt Gwen. Melanie almost slammed the drawer shut, but something made her hesitate. Pulling it out with shaking hands, she read the card over again.

Slowly she walked out of the closet and over to her desk. She sat down, only to come face-to-face with the small framed print of Venice Beach she'd bought for Jesse in L.A. She had propped the watercolor against the wall, waiting for her chance to give it to him. Now she slapped it facedown and took out a sheet of stationery, centering it in front of her.

She fussed with her fountain pen, stared out the window . . . but a second glance at the overturned print convinced her. Her fingers tightened on the barrel as she touched the pen's nib to the paper.

Dear Aunt Gwen . . .

"So are you going to tell me what we're doing here?" Miguel asked edgily, and Leah could tell by his voice he knew something was up.

She stirred the floating whipped cream into her hot chocolate. "We need to talk," she told him.

"What about?"

Leah glanced uneasily around the ice cream parlor, where they'd found seats on opposite sides of a quiet booth. At that time of day—an hour before dinner on a chilly Monday—the restaurant was nearly deserted. The reason Leah had chosen it, though, was because the place meant nothing to her. She and Miguel had never been there before and if, after today, it was full of bad memories, she never had to come back.

"Is it about the wedding?" he prompted.

"Sort of." She took a deep breath, fixed her gaze on his brown eyes, and charged recklessly ahead. "I love you, Miguel. But I'm still afraid we might be making a big mistake."

He didn't flinch. "How so?"

"I've been talking to my mother about marriage. Not you and I getting married," she hurried to add. "Just in general. And some of the things she said have really got me worried. We'll both be giving up so much—what if we're unhappy and blame each

190

other? And my parents were together *eight years* before they got married. I feel like I know you better than anyone, but . . ."

Miguel's expression hadn't changed in the slightest, but Leah trailed off anyway, too confused to continue. She felt she was betraying him more with every word. But if she didn't speak up now, wasn't she betraying them both?

"In other words, you have doubts," he said flatly.

Her heart ached at the thought of hurting him, but how could she say she didn't? "Yes. I'm sorry."

To her amazement, Miguel smiled a little. "Don't be. I haven't slept right since the night I proposed."

"You . . . what?"

"I love you, too," he told her. "But it's all the things you just said. Plus my mom still needs me. And, well, to tell you the truth, I don't think she's going to be too happy to see me get married."

"You mean to see you get married outside of the church," Leah guessed. She didn't need to look any further than her own family to know the difficulties she and Miguel would face in that regard.

Miguel seemed relieved that she'd said it first. "She's going to flip. And I can't help wondering . . . if I'm really ready to get married, should I be this worried about my mother's reaction?"

"I know what you mean," Leah said, playing with her spoon. "My parents are going to have heart attacks too. And my mom, well, she kind of asked me if I was thinking about getting married . . . and I kind of told her I wasn't. I feel like a criminal."

She looked into his eyes and saw her own anguish reflected there. He started to say something, then closed his mouth. Leaning forward, he reached for her hand and tried again.

"Do you want to call this off?" he asked, his voice not much more than a whisper.

"Do you?"

Neither one breathed as they searched each other's faces.

"I don't *want* to," he said. "But if we did, we could stop worrying about telling our parents, and where we'll live, and how we're going to make a living, and whether or not you'll ever go to college, and just, well, a lot of things."

"So you're saying it would be *easier* to drop it."

"No, I—I don't know what I'm saying, Leah. It's just that if neither one of us is sure about this, it might be smarter to wait."

"Wouldn't that be going back on our promise?"

Miguel shrugged. "I haven't told anyone. Have you?"

"No."

"Then our only promise is to each other. If we both want to, we can change our minds."

He sounded as if he had half changed his already. Leah felt a lump lodge in her throat even as she acknowledged that she had too. But while it was one thing to know that she wanted out, it still hurt to hear *him* say it.

"If we . . . if we don't get married," she said haltingly, "then I will go to college in the fall. And if you stay here, I'm afraid, well . . . Long-distance relationships never work."

"That's just not true," he said, shaking his head. "Besides, we wouldn't have to live in different cities for longer than a school year. Maybe only a semester. And you'd be coming home for vacations, right? If we can't get through that, we shouldn't be getting married anyway."

It was done, then. Neither one of them had said so in so many words, but they could read it in each other's eyes. "I guess you're right."

"Of course I'm right. Don't misunderstand me, Leah—I still want to marry you someday. But when we walk down that aisle together, I want it to be with no doubt."

She nodded blindly as hot tears ran down her cheeks.

Miguel slipped out of his bench and came around to hers, sliding in beside her. Putting an arm across her shoulders, he brought his lips to her ear.

"Someday, when we're ready, I want to propose again—with a *real* ring, a diamond one. And we'll have a real engagement and tell the entire world."

"Okay," she agreed, barely able to speak.

193

She knew she should be relieved, but all she felt was sadness. Maybe she and Miguel had no business getting married, but the decision not to do so still felt like a terrible loss. So many different things could happen in the future, and with this engagement called off there was no guarantee of another one. The two of them could grow apart, he could fall in love with someone else . . .

Miguel kissed her wet cheek, and when she turned her head to face him, she saw his eyes were full as well. Tears pooled in his dark lashes until they overflowed and dropped onto the seat between them. She nuzzled her face against his, mingling their tears.

"I love you so much," he murmured against her mouth. "I don't want to lose you, Leah."

Somehow the words eased the weight on her heart.

"You're not going to lose me," she promised, squeezing him tighter. "You just go ahead and try."

"That's a chili cheese dog, an order of frings, and a chocolate shakeosaurus to go," Gail called back over her shoulder. She totaled the order on the cash register and began collecting the customer's money.

"I've got it!" Nicole sang out, scurrying to assemble the food.

That Monday evening was her first time working behind the counter, and she was determined to im-

194

press Mr. Roarke with her efficiency. Putting the orders together wasn't as good as working the register, but it was the next easiest job—and way more desirable than cleaning the bathrooms. Nicole's plan was to make herself indispensable, to get a lock on the position for future shifts.

"I need a chili cheese dog and an order of frings," she yelled through the pass-through window to the kitchen. Pausing just long enough to be sure that Ajax had heard her, she grabbed a giant paper cup from the dispenser and began filling it with ice cream for the shakeosaurus—the most enormous shake in the Wienerageous arsenal.

"Frings up!" Ajax shouted back. "Chili cheese dog up!"

Nicole put the milk shake on the blender, then snapped open a fresh paper bag. The food she'd asked for rested in the stainless steel bins of the pass-through. She picked up the order of frings—a paper tray filled half with onion rings and half with french fries—and set it gently in the bottom of the bag, taking care not to spill anything. The chili cheese dog fit in beside that, chili side up. Ketchup, salt, napkins—Nicole made sure she included it all before she closed up the bag with three crisp folds. Setting the food aside, she took the shake off the blender, checked the outside of the cup for drips, and snapped on a plastic lid.

"Order up!" she said, bringing the completed order to Gail.

"Thank you for eating at Wienerageous," Gail told her customer as she passed the food across the counter to the woman. "Come again—and bring a friend!"

"Uh-huh," the woman said with a weak smile. She took her bag and left, clearing the way for the only other person standing in line.

"Welcome to Wienerageous, where our smiles are contagious!" Gail chirped as if oblivious to the fact that her new customer was a very cute teenage guy.

Maybe counter is better than register after all, Nicole thought, cringing. Putting the orders together required a little more running around, but at least she didn't have to talk to the customers.

The guy barely seemed to notice Gail, however, as he scanned the overhead menu. "Yeah. Give me two chili dogs, a large fries, a Bodacious Burger, a large Coke, and an apple pie."

Nicole's eyes widened at the size of the order, but Gail didn't miss a beat. "Would you like a slice of our cheesecake with that? It's really good."

The guy shrugged. "All right. Why not?"

"Is that for here or to go?"

"For here."

Gail rang up his order as Nicole put the food together, this time on a tray.

I can't believe that one regular-sized person can eat so much! she thought as she hurried around. *Leave it to Gail to sell him a cheesecake too.*

Her cousin was in top form again that day, kissing Mr. Roarke's butt and being extra-sweet to all the customers. Every stupid slogan was recited with gusto, every smile was ultrabright. If Nicole hadn't seen Gail's darker side with her own eyes she never would have believed that the apparently model employee in front of her was actually the most accomplished actress on Earth.

Nicole finished off the tray with a large Coke and brought it to the counter.

"Here you go," she said, starting to push it across. But a sideways glance at the cash register stopped her with her hands still on the tray.

"That can't be right," she told Gail in a low voice.

Maybe she'd never worked the register, but Nicole had paid for enough fast food in her life to know there was no way that huge order cost $2.54. Gail couldn't have rung up even half the stuff on the tray.

"It's fine," Gail whispered back. "Don't sweat it."

The guy she was waiting on looked back and forth between them. "Is there a problem?"

Nicole was certain he knew exactly what the problem was.

"No problem," said Gail.

Nicole tried to smile, but she was starting to panic. "You rang it up wrong, Gail," she whispered. "You must have."

"It looks all right to me." The guy reached for his tray.

Gail reached for it too, pulling it from Nicole's fingers and pushing it into his.

"Cute-guy discount," she explained in a mischievous whisper.

She winked at her customer, who smiled before he walked off to find a table.

"Gail, you can't do that!" Nicole whispered desperately. "If you don't charge the right amount, you're going to get us both fired. No free food for anyone, ever. Remember?"

Gail glanced right and left. They were alone behind the counter.

"Nobody's looking," she whispered back. "It's not a big deal unless you make it one."

Nicole stared, her heart pounding. Of course it was a big deal! It was stealing!

But what could she do about it? She couldn't tell Mr. Roarke, that was for sure. She'd have to handle Gail herself somehow. But how?

Turning reluctantly from the register, she started toward the end of the counter. *I'll go get a towel and clean something. That'll keep me busy a minute while I figure out what to do.*

She reached the corner at the counter's end in a daze. *I suppose I could pay for that free food myself . . .*

But while that would ease her conscience, it wouldn't solve the problem—not unless she could also convince Gail not to do it again.

Nicole made the turn to walk into the kitchen

and almost collided with Mr. Roarke. Her boss was standing just around the corner at the end of the pass-through wall, barely out of sight.

"Whoops! Excuse me, Mr. Roarke," Nicole said nervously. "I was just going to get a, uh . . ."

Her boss's small eyes glared, hard with disapproval, and Nicole's breath caught in her chest. Had he seen? She looked backward over her shoulder. Gail's register was right in her line of sight.

He was spying, she realized, dizzy with her own pulse. *He just saw everything!*

And when she dared to face him again, his expression left no doubt.

She and Gail were busted.

About the Author

Laura Peyton Roberts holds an M.A. in English from San Diego State University. A native Californian, she lives with her husband in San Diego.